DEAD IN L.A.
LOU HARPER

L.A. Paranormal 1 & 2

First published in the United States in2012 by Harper Books
First Edition

This book is a work of fiction. The names, characters, places, and incidents are products of the writer's imagination or have been used fictitiously and are not to be construed as real. Any resemblance to persons, living or dead, actual events, locale or organizations is entirely coincidental.

Copyright © 2012 Lou Harper
Cover Art by Lou Harper Copyright 2012

All rights reserved. No part of this book may be used or reproduced in any manner whatsoever without written permission, except in the case of brief quotations embodied in critical articles and reviews.

ISBN: 1481176889
ISBN-13: 978-1481176880

DEDICATION

Pork Chop, it's all your fault.

DEAD IN THE HILLS

Chapter One

It's the randomness of things that scares me the most—not knowing what fate or blind chance have in store. Your whole life can turn on a dime when you least expect it. I'd known that for a fact, and hated the out-of-control feeling. But after a rough year of it, I was finally on the mend. I thought if I kept my head down, and my life complications-free, I'd be fine. So when I put up flyers at nearby campuses, a roommate was all I was looking for. Preferably a socially inept nerd. Someone to pay half the rent and cause no trouble.

Barely a day later, the first email inquiry arrived from someone called Lea. I sent back a brief reply telling her to stop by after three. If she didn't mind sharing an apartment with a guy, I had nothing against her.

Five after three the bell rang, and I found a skinny guy at my doorstep. The first thing that struck me about him was how his blond hair stuck out in every direction—as if it was trying to escape his scalp. The second thing I noted was a pair of cornflower eyes.

They beamed at me with unwarranted cheer. "Hi, I'm here about the room." With his smooth skin and guileless gaze he seemed as young and innocent as a freshly laid egg.

He had me confused and I made no secret of it. "I was expecting a girl—Lea." I pronounced it *Lay-uh*, like a normal person would.

He flashed a smile. "Oh, that's me. Leander Thorne, Lea for short." He said it like *Lee*. "Rhymes with tea," he added, and held his hand out.

There I was, having known him for five seconds, and he

already had me mixed up. It should've been a clue, but hindsight never needs bifocals. I shrugged off the confusion and marched on. "Jon Cooper. No *H*."

We shook hands and I invited him in. While I showed him around, Leander—what were his parents thinking?—hung on my every word.

"And this is your room," I said, concluding the tour.

He stepped inside and spun around on his heels. "Very nice. I love the color."

The landlady had given me a break on the first month's rent when I offered to repaint the rooms myself. I didn't know why I'd chosen that sunny yellow for this one, but I thought it suited him. Of course, I didn't tell him that. Instead, I stuck to business. While he inspected the room, I laid out the facts. "There are house rules. My name's on the lease, and I'll put your ass out on the street if you break them. No loud music, at any time. No wild parties or other crap that would annoy the neighbors. No pets. And for goodness sake, if you have friends coming by to pick you up, have them walk up to the door. That honking on the street business is fucking obnoxious."

"That won't be a problem. I don't have friends," he said it in an off-handed way, while scrutinizing the deep corners of an open dresser drawer.

You had to be a cold-hearted bastard like me not to be affected. *With a name like Leander? Surprise,* I thought, but what I said was, "You're young. I'm sure you'll pick up a few. How old are you anyway, eighteen?"

"Twenty-two!"

I swallowed a laugh at the sight of him puffing out his narrow chest. Yeah, you could say I liked him right off, and he seemed suitably nerdy too.

"Good for you." I slapped him on the back, but grabbed his shoulder before he launched face forward. "C'mon, let me show you the half-bath."

I maneuvered him to the door at the far wall. The room behind wasn't much—only a toilet and a sink, but it would give him added privacy, and it also meant I'd have the main bathroom mostly to myself.

"Cool," he said absently and tilted his head like a bird as he looked at me. "I saw an empty book case in the living room, and I have a few books…"

This further sign of nerdishness brightened my mood. "Sure, it's yours. Anything else?"

"No."

"So you want the place?"

He nodded vigorously.

I figured this set up would work out pretty well for me. I was six foot three and in the neighborhood of two hundred pounds. I could probably bench press the guy, even with my bad shoulder. He'd be no problem.

***

Luckily for Leander, I was home when he arrived with the rental van and could help him unload. His "few" books made up two-thirds of his earthly possessions. They took over the entire bookcase with several boxes left over.

"Have you read them all?" I asked. I hoped he wasn't one of those hoarder types.

"Of course." He collapsed into a chair. I was impressed he'd managed to get those boxes into the truck by himself. Books are heavy, and he wasn't exactly brawny.

"Then why keep them?" I read books too, but I didn't collect them.

He looked at me like I was an alien. "Why wouldn't I?"

"You already know how they end, so what's the point?"

He gave me a wounded look. "You don't read books to know the ending, but for the whole experience. I re-read my favorites at least once a year." He gazed at the bookcase with a rapturous smile. "And they make me feel at home."

Yeah, a regular egghead, all right. That was the most conversation we had for a while. Secretly, I enjoyed having another person around. Solitude had never suited me. I liked finding him on the living room sofa, nose in a book when I got home from school, or simply hearing the noises as he puttered around. The apartment even smelled different with him in it. Leander radiated an easy warmth, but I didn't want him to get the impression we were pals. He had a vague stray cat vibe about him, and I had no plans to play the Good Samaritan.

At any rate, fall semester started and I got busy. And anxious. Going back to school had sounded like a good idea when I signed up, but now doubts and fears sat like a heavy meal in the pit of my stomach. What if I was wrong? I could end up penniless and unemployed. Being older than most students gave me an intense feeling of not belonging. I was a burned-out twenty-eight, feeling decades older, while they flitted around me with their unhatched lives, full of hope and promise. They irritated the hell out of me. I wanted to shake them and tell them to stop being so happy, it would go to shit in no time.

I hadn't always been such a cheerful bastard, but insomnia and nightmares had haunted me since the doctors had taken me off the good drugs. On this particular night I dreamt I was driving a car, but unable to steer or step on the brakes. I half-woke before crashing, kicked off my blankets, and went back to sleep.

Next I knew I was staring at a carton of milk.

"Jon, you okay?" Leander asked.

I gaped at him. "Huh?"

"You look like you've just found the gates to another dimension in the crisper."

I stared at him for a second, then back at the milk. Apparently, I was standing at the open fridge door, wearing only my boxers. *Fucking great.* I shut the fridge and pulled myself together. "I had trouble sleeping. Did I wake you?"

The clock on the wall showed five past midnight.

His gaze snapped from my midsection to my face, and a frown of concern ruffled his face. "Nah, I was reading. I'm a night owl. Sit. I'll make something that'll help you sleep."

I bet it would be herbal tea. He had stacks of the stuff and Ramen noodles in his side of the kitchen cabinet. Not much else. I didn't care for tea, but was too off-balance to object. So I sat and wondered how long I'd been sleepwalking, and whether I'd given myself away. It was bad enough that I was cracking up; I didn't need anyone else to know it too.

He put the kettle on and pulled out another chair. "You go to PCC, right? What do you study?"

PCC is what everyone calls Pasadena City College. I scratched my chin. The scrape of stubble seemed to echo in the quietness of the kitchen. "Art."

His eyes got big. "Really?"

"I don't look the part, right?"

"No! You look good." I swear, he blushed. "Ehrm, what I mean is, artists are like anyone else. Physically. Well, otherwise too. Mostly." He bit his lip. "What did you do before?"

"Construction."

He nodded. I'm sure he had an easier time imagining me in a hard hat than with an easel. "So, what made you go back to school?"

"I needed a change." That was the understatement of the year. After a year of depression I needed to get away from everything that reminded me of my late wife, Alicia, or I would've jumped off a bridge, and it's not that easy to find a suitable one in L.A. Most of them are over freeways. Causing a pile-up wasn't my wish.

He stared at me expectantly, so I added, "I had an accident, and it fucked up my shoulder. I had to find a new career."

"And you decided to be an artist. How awesome!" He

didn't just say it to be polite either. His smile shone as if I'd revealed a precious secret.

I had to quickly disillusion him about my awesomeness. "Not exactly. PCC has all kinds of vocational training courses. I planned on taking a practical major like Automotive Technology or Electricity. But I made the mistake of telling my advisor about drawing—it's my hobby—and she asked me to demonstrate. Before I knew what hit me, she had me sign up for advertising design." Seeing Leander's attentive gaze, I realized I was babbling on like an old geezer. Being tired did that to me.

"What's wrong with advertising design?"

"It's flaky. The world will always need electricians. They make a good living." I still could hardly believe I let Mrs. Matthews talk me into an art major. There was something about motherly women I couldn't say no to. And by motherly, I didn't mean like my own mother, who was as warm as the North Pole.

What Leander did next took me totally by surprise. He reached out and put his hand on mine. I couldn't even search his downcast eyes for explanation. His touch was both soft and firm, sending electrical signals through my body, waking up cravings I didn't want awake. I sat frozen like a rabbit in front of a snake. I wanted to yank my hand away but that would've looked stupid. Fortunately, the shriek of the kettle broke the moment.

"You'll be all right," he said getting up and turning to the stove. "You're not an alcoholic, right?" he asked over his shoulder.

"No, I'm not," I replied startled by the strangeness of the question.

"Good."

While he busied himself, I rubbed the back of my hand and wondered when I'd become such a wimp. I needed to get a grip on myself.

He put a steaming mug in front of me. "Chamomile Toddy. My Grams's recipe."

"Grams?"

"Grandma. She raised me after my parents died. Careful, it's hot."

I got the impression he didn't feel like talking about his dead any more than I did. Most of all, I didn't want to know intimate details about him. Not getting involved with other people and their lives was part of my no complications policy.

"So what do you study?" I asked and took a cautious sip. It tasted atrocious, with the saving grace of rum.

"Oh. Nothing. I'm not a student."

This news surprised me—it hadn't occurred to me he'd be anything else. "So what do you do?"

He bit his lip again. If he didn't stop, they'd chap. "I'm…uhm…a psychic."

Oh great, a whacko. I did my best to keep my face straight. "You tell fortunes?" I asked politely. The proper way to deal with nut jobs is to pretend you take them seriously.

"No. Not like that. I find things."

The plot thickened. "What things?"

"Whatever people lose. Cats, dogs, keys, whatnot."

Sounded hinky as hell. "You can make a living with it?"

He shrugged. "Well, I've only been doing it professionally for a short time. I also do audience work."

"Audience what?"

"You know, sitting in the audience for TV shows."

"I thought people lined up to be on those."

"Sure, the popular ones, but even those tend to have a portion of professionals. A paid audience will laugh even when the jokes are not funny. I've signed up with a casting agency as an extra, and they send me to those. It doesn't pay a whole lot but it's better than nothing."

I started to have an inkling he'd be far more trouble than I'd thought. He'd better pay his half of the rent on time. I wasn't running a charity for overgrown orphans, no matter how big and blue their eyes were.

We sat in silence while I sipped my drink. I was getting used to the flavor and starting to feel the effects. I knew he was studying me, trying to measure me up. I did the same to him. He had an open face, freckles across his nose. His curvy lips seemed ready to smile at the slightest provocation.

"Leander." I rolled the name on my tongue.

"Mmm?"

"What kind of name is it anyway?"

"My mother named me after a character in Greek mythology. Leander fell in love with Hero, a priestess of Aphrodite. He swam a river every night to be with her. She lit a candle to guide him. Than one stormy night the wind blew the candle out and he drowned. She threw herself into the waves to be with him forever."

I digested the story for a moment. "That's just dumb."

"Dumb?" His eyes opened wide with disbelief.

I might have offended him, but stuck by my opinion. "She should've used a proper lamp, or at least a torch, and he should have taken a rowboat. Even the ancient Greeks had torches and boats, didn't they?"

He rolled his eyes. "Tragic love stories are the most romantic. Like Romeo and Juliet, don't you think?"

I hated that stupid play. "No. Young people die for no good reason, because their families are assholes. It's not romantic to me." I knew as I said the words that I was taking it too personally. Alicia's family and mine lurked in the back of my mind.

His lips curved down. "Sorry."

And now I felt like an ass. "Don't be. It's my problem, not yours." I put the empty cup down and stretched. "I should give the sandman another chance. Good night." I pushed myself off the table.

"Sweet dreams."

Fat chance of that. Back in bed, I closed my eyes, and Alicia's face floated into my mind, but I didn't want to think of her, so I concentrated on Leander's instead. Maybe if I counted the freckles... I drifted off before five.

***

A few days later I lounged in my room in the company of a three-pound art history book. I praised my foresight in buying a used copy—it had been half the price and the important parts were already highlighted. I was taking classes for fifteen credits total, but only English and Art History posed an actual challenge. The design and drawing classes turned out to be more fun than work. They still took up time, and I had a busy schedule. Tuesdays were murder with classes from morning till night, but I had the weekends and Wednesday afternoons free.

Timid knocking at the door of my room got my attention.

"What is it?" I yelled out.

"It's me, Leander," came the voice from the other side.

Nobody could see me roll my eyes. "I guessed that much. Come in for God's sake."

The door creaked open and his messy blond head peeked in. Did he own a comb?

"Jon?"

"Yes?"

"Can I ask a favor? I'll understand if you say no, after all you barely know me, and I wouldn't ask, but it's sort of urgent..."

I was losing patience. "Spit it out already."

"Can I borrow your car? Mine won't start, and I have a paying job. It's not far, right up the hills. I promise I'll be careful."

There was no way in hell I would let him or anyone else drive my car, but seeing the pleading look on his face, I couldn't say no either. "I'll drive you."

He brightened up immediately. "Will you? Thanks!"

"Fine, fine." I pulled my shoes on. "You ready?"

"I just need my bag."

"What do you keep in that?" I asked as we got into the car and he planted the green canvas satchel in his lap.

"Maps."

"Why don't you use the GPS on your phone?"

He shook his head. "I tried. It doesn't work."

I decided against asking him to explain. Maybe I should've. "So where are we going, and why?"

He showed me the notepaper with the address on it. "Go up on Lake and take a right when we get to the street. The house is supposed to be on the left side."

"And why?" I reminded him.

"My client is Mrs. Bowman, who wants me to find her son. He disappeared sometime yesterday, and she's very worried."

"How old?'

"Seventeen."

"Ah, a teenager." The whole thing sounded screwy to me, and it also started to make me feel uncomfortable. Monkeying around with missing cats was one thing, but people were a different matter. For the time being, I decided to keep my mouth shut and my eyes open.

The Bowmans lived in a nice house on the good side of Lake Avenue, north of the country club. Big old trees shaded the whole neighborhood, their branches full of squawking feral parrots.

When Leander thanked me for the ride, on a whim I offered to join him inside. I didn't feel like waiting at the curb or coming back later, but abandoning him there would've been rude. Most of all, I was dying to know what he did. I wouldn't have been offended if he'd turned me down, but he didn't. He even gave me a grateful smile.

Mary and George Bowman seemed like an otherwise nice couple strung out after a sleepless night. I knew that feeling. Mary kept clasping and unclasping her hands. The gaze she pinned on Leander was full of fear and hope. Her husband stood stiffly and eyed us with barely veiled contempt. After hurried introductions, Leander asked if he could have something personal of their son's.

"Clothes he wore last would be best," he said.

Mary hurried away, and back a minute later, clutching a wrinkled T-shirt. "This was in his room, tossed on the bed," she explained.

"That's perfect, thank you. Mind if I go ito your backyard? I'll be able to concentrate better there." Leander motioned toward the open bay windows.

The baffled Bowmans agreed. Leander drew me aside and whispered in my ear, "Their emotions are too distracting. Keep them in here, please?"

Suddenly, I felt like a conspirator in a plan I didn't understand. I nodded anyway, and turned to our hosts, while he marched outside. From inside they watched as he sat in the grass and held the T-shirt to his face.

"When did Jeremy disappear?" I asked Mary, mainly for distraction.

Her eyes flickered to me. "Not sure. We didn't get home till late, but I talked to Jeremy on the phone at around two. He said he might go over to his friend's."

"Did he?"

"No. We called all his friends and talked to our neighbors too, but no one knew anything. Mrs. Holsman, who lives at the corner, recommended Leander—she said he'd found her dog, Sparky."

George made a derisive noise. "And you listen to that old

bat. What's he doing now?" The last part referred to Leander, who took a map out of his bag and unfolded it over the grass. We held our breaths as he leaned forward and touched a finger to its surface.

Loud knocking made us jump. Mary rushed to open the door, with George right on her heels. I drifted after them to see a uniformed policeman standing there. After identifying himself as Officer Carter, he informed the Bowmans that Jeremy's car had been found at the top of Lake Street. A patrol officer spotted it because of a broken window.

"He's right here," Leander said behind us.

We whirled around and saw him holding up a map with a red X on it. I looked closer. The mark sat right on top of a trail—one that started not far from the place where Jeremy had parked.

George rushed off to make phone calls and organize a search party, and Mary disappeared somewhere else. We were left with a distrustful Officer Carter, who wanted to know who we were and what we were doing there. We told him, but the information didn't endear us to him one bit.

To my relief, Mary came back. She thrust a folded up check in Leander's hand. "Is he alive?" Her eyes shone with tears about to burst.

"Sorry, I don't know," Leander said in a small voice.

I took his elbow. "We should go."

Chapter Two

I didn't know what to think about the whole thing. I considered myself a sensible person, not susceptible to hocus-pocus, so I searched for a logical explanation. Maybe Leander had overheard Officer Carter, and made a wild guess. And it was yet to be seen if he'd come even close to getting it right.

I glanced sideways at Leander, who slumped in his seat, staring out the window. I'd gotten used to him being chipper, so this change of mood seemed odd.

"What's wrong?" I asked.

He shook his head. "I lied to her. He's dead." Dark shadows circled his eyes—they hadn't been there an hour ago.

"How do you know?"

"I just do. He went biking on one of those narrow trails, going downhill too fast. An animal spooked him. He lost his balance and fell to his death."

I couldn't hold my incredulity in any longer. "You can't possibly know that."

"I do. Something else too. There was a girl he had a crush on, but she liked someone else."

His obvious distress rattled me, and maybe that's why I said what I did. "Psychics aren't real."

"Are you saying I'm only a figment of your imagination?" His eyes flashed and bitterness sharpened his voice.

"You know what I mean," I said stubbornly.

He pressed his lips into a thin line and turned away. He might've been a con artist, but I couldn't see it. So, he must've truly believed this psychic nonsense. That meant he was a nut, and I'd already known that much. I still had issues with him taking money from distressed parents, but seeing the tense lines of his shoulders, I decided not to bring that up.

I glanced at my watch. It was almost five. "Look, I need to go by the campus, but I'll drop you off at home first."

"No. I can walk home from there. It's not far."

"You could wait for me. I won't be long."

"I really need a walk." The strain in his voice was plain to hear.

I relented. "All right."

***

I had a quick meeting with my drawing prof, who grilled me about my long-term plans. I admitted not having any beyond getting a paying job at some point. The sooner the better. She tutted but let me go. I headed straight home but found the apartment dark and empty. I told myself Leander was a big boy who could take care of himself. He could've stopped at a bar, gone shopping, whatever. Not my business. I fixed myself dinner, then settled on the sofa with the art history book. After reading the same page four times without absorbing a single word, I slammed it shut and switched on the TV.

Leander drifted in around eight.

"Where have you been?" I snapped at him, surprising both of us.

He blinked at me several times before finding his voice. "In the park, unwinding. Why?"

"Erhm, nothing. You could've called."

"What for? Anyway, I don't know your number."

"We need to fix that. There could be apartment emergencies."

"Sure," he said, starting toward his room.

"Have you had dinner yet?" I called after him.

He stopped and shrugged. "I'll have toast."

Seriously? He needed real food—he was skinny. "I made too much spaghetti. It's in the kitchen—help yourself."

"You can have that for lunch tomorrow."

"Just shut up and eat, okay?"

He pursed his lips and the usual sparkle returned to his eyes. "Yes, boss."

His smile made me completely miss the fact that I'd just started feeding the stray cat. Later we watched TV together. Jeremy Bowman made the ten o'clock news, although they didn't identify him by name, only as "local youth." It had taken the rescue team over an hour to recover his body from a ravine. There was no mention of how they'd found him to begin with.

***

The next day I took a look at Leander's car, a battered silver Honda, at least a decade old. It simply needed a new battery. We took care of it and Leander had his mobility back. For a couple of weeks our lives went on as before.

Since the beginning of football season, Sunday nights had found us together in front of the TV. We had beer and snacks, and spent a couple of hours shouting at the players. Perfect way to finish up a weekend, if you ask me. Leander's interest in football came as a shocker, since he otherwise preferred cooking shows, especially the ones where chefs competed against each other.

"Why are you watching those?" I asked him once. "You hardly ever cook."

"It's the drama," he replied.

In my opinion, football beats *Iron Chef* for drama, any day. Supposedly he watched *Project Runway* for the same reason. He couldn't have been more obviously gay if he'd tried. I'd always preferred masculine men, but his boyishness had a certain appeal. Especially after a few beers. Yeah okay, he was totally hot, but without the self-awareness that made most guys like him unappealing to me. He still wasn't my type—as I firmly reminded myself.

We took turns supplying the booze and snacks. I stuck to

standard fare but Leander tended to bring weird things, like blue cheese popcorn—probably whatever had caught his eye at Trader Joe's. And fancy microbrewery beers that must've cost him a pretty penny.

To be honest, I preferred not having to watch the games alone, because football is meant to be enjoyed in company. Otherwise it's like masturbation—it gets you off but it's not half as much fun as sex with another person. I should know. Even so, watching football with Leander was an unorthodox experience.

"Run twenty-four, run!" he shouted at the screen.

I had no idea why. "Which team are you cheering for?"

"The one in red shirts."

"You mean jerseys?"

He shrugged. "Sure."

I had to ask. "Why?"

"Because they're the underdogs, the ones who get beamed down to alien planets only to die for dramatic effect." He spoke with conviction, like any of it made sense. In his head it probably did.

No, I was *not* going to encourage him. But there was one thing I needed to point out. "Twenty-four didn't have the ball."

"So? There's way too big a deal made of that ball, don't you think? I like to immerse myself in the full experience." He grinned like a fool.

I narrowed my eyes with suspicion. "Do you even understand the rules?" I wouldn't have put it past him to watch the game only for the guys in tight pants.

"Sure I do! It's exactly like Quidditch but without brooms."

Well, I deserved that for asking. I shook my head and took refuge in beer. Swilling the bitter liquid around in my mouth, I inspected the label on the bottle. "Why are you wasting your money on this pricey stuff? Cheap beer would get you the same buzz."

"Would it?" His grin morphed into one somebody else would've called impish. Not me though.

I took a closer look at the label. "What, 9% alcohol by volume? Are you trying to get me drunk? I'm sorry, but you'll need something stronger." I was little buzzed, though. Just enough to fall into the blue of his eyes.

"I'll keep that in mind." He smiled as he leaned forward with the half-empty bowl of popcorn in his hands.

His short-sleeved T-shirt was black, and the thin cotton hugging him tight stood in stark contrast with his milky-white skin and the blond fuzz on his arms. They invited to touch, so I did. Brushing the back of my fingers against the naked flesh was almost innocent, an act of curiosity. I petted the downy fuzz against the grain. The bowl clunked on the table, and Leander turned to me. His face was so close to mine, his eyes became a blur. I smelled beer, soap, and a hint of perspiration. So real, so alive, it took my breath away. We moved incrementally, a tilt of heads, eyelids fluttering closed, lips drawn to the other's by the magnetic force of desire. He tasted bitter and salty, an answer to my late night cravings.

The way he kissed you'd think he'd been as famished as I was. The black shirt peeled off to reveal more paleness. Even my untanned skin seemed dark in comparison. *Lily white*, I thought, but the insistence with which he pushed his hands under my clothes didn't suit the virtuous image of a flower. Soon we lay on the sofa shirtless, jeans around our ankles, limbs tangled. I took greedy possession of his body, and he gave it with abandon. There was nothing shy or hesitant about how he dug his hands into my back, or the way he thrust his groin against mine.

I forgot my fears and sorrows and lost myself in the urgency of the moment. We didn't talk and the few words uttered were nonsensical. For a while everything was so very simple, the whole world consisted of only the two of us, working for a common goal. Release came in a sticky rush.

Dead In L.A.

> Suddenly spent and tired, I stretched out and closed my eyes for a second.

***

When I opened them again, it was Monday morning and I was lying in my bed. I had to have gotten there under my own power, but I didn't remember. Sleepwalking had its upsides, I noted. I might have been a head case, but at least a practical one. Unfortunately, memories of the night before floated back and they gave me the hangover the beer hadn't. Breaking my routine, I took off to school without breakfast and had lunch at the cafeteria. After the afternoon class I spent time in the library and in the studio.

I needed to sort my head out. I couldn't afford the risk of getting mixed up with someone. Friends and lovers were more dangerous than muggers. They could hurt you in ways strangers couldn't, and I was still bleeding. What had happened had been a mistake but entirely mine. I had to explain it to Leander without causing harm.

When I finally did go home, I found Leander in front of the TV, watching a cooking show and eating noodle soup.

I decided to cut to the chase. "Hi. Got a minute?"

He put the bowl down and muted the TV. The expectant look in his eyes made me feel like an even bigger heel. I hardened myself. "Listen, about last night—"

His face darkened. "It was a mistake, you had too much to drink, and it's not me, it's you." His delivery was flatter than a radio weather report.

My practiced speech went out the window. "What?"

"Isn't that what you were going to say?"

"Well, yeah, but—"

"I'm young, not stupid. Did I leave anything out? You're not really gay?" Right there, a sneer peeped out from behind the careful facade. I didn't like it.

"I'm a hundred percent gay," I said indignantly.

"Good." As his muscles relaxed, the pinched look left his face, but not the guardedness.

He reached for the remote, but I wasn't done. "Listen, it's really not you. I just don't want to get involved right now. I'd be lousy at a relationship, trust me."

"Getting your rocks off on the couch does not a relationship make. I'd like us to be friends though."

Friends? Such a big word. People use it too frivolously. You might have one or two genuine friends in your whole life. The rest are acquaintances. Leander and I were friendly, not friends. If he breezed out my life tomorrow, I'd survive. I kept these thoughts to myself though, and nodded. "Okay. Friends."

His lips quirked. "Who now and then have hot sex on the couch."

"I don't think that's a good idea."

"Just think about it," he said un-muting the TV, and reaching for the bowl.

"Sure. You know, you can't eat Ramen soup at every meal. It's not healthy."

"There's an egg in it," he pointed it out.

I wasn't impressed. Friends don't let friends eat instant noodles, I decided.

Chapter Three

I made it my job to ensure Leander at least had a full breakfast every morning. I always whipped one up for myself—most important meal of the day, after all. Doing it for two made no difference. I had him chip in for groceries, and do the dishes afterwards. Of course, he had to get up earlier than he'd been used to—something he grumbled about. The way I saw it, he'd get over it sooner or later.

"You could at least sleep in on weekends," he griped on one fine Saturday morning.

"I did," I replied and piled sausages on his plate.

"Nine a.m. doesn't count as sleeping in." He glared at me from under a mess of blond hair. I had to resist the urge to smooth it out for him.

So instead I started on my eggs. We ate in peace and quiet for a while. Leander happened to be an astonishingly slow eater. I was mopping up my plate with a piece of toast before he finished half of his food. However, he drank coffee like a pro. After the first cup he became chatty.

"So, how's school?" he asked.

"Fine."

He glared at me. "Could you be a wee bit more detailed?"

I pushed my plate away. "English isn't as bad as I expected. According to my professor, I write like Mickey Spillane, whoever that is. Art History's all right. In Design class we're learning about negative space, and my drawing instructor thinks I should take Life Drawing next semester." I cracked a smile thinking of the spirited old broad, who seemed to think I had talent.

"That's with models, right?"

"Yup."

"What do you draw now?"

"Still lifes. We moved from geometric shapes to objects," I said, eyeing the way the morning light slanted through the glass salt and pepper shakers. I nudged a small spoon to the left. "I like working with charcoal the most."

"Why?"

"I don't know. I guess it's the shades of gray and the softness. Or maybe I just like to get my hands dirty."

I stood and put my plate in the sink. I should've gotten a start on my English essay, but instead I grabbed one of my many drawing pads, sat back down and began to sketch. When you look at an ordinary object up close, you notice its details and it becomes unique. Transferring all that onto a piece of paper posed a challenge and getting it right was gratifying. On a quiet Saturday morning I could even forget about it being such a trivial thing to do.

Leander remained blessedly quiet while finishing his eggs. After clearing every last crumb off his plate he came around and stood next to me. "Hey, that's really good," he said, leaning forward. His bony hip pressed against my arm. Body heat surrounded him like a seductive aura, brushing against my skin.

"Dishes?" I reminded him.

"Slave driver," he said with a sigh, and detached himself from me, to my relief.

While he cleared the table and put on a fresh pot of coffee, I flipped to a blank page, but before I could start, the sound of knocking came from the door. Sharp and insistent, it demanded attention. I pushed my chair back. "I'll get it."

Opening the door I saw a stocky man in his forties with thinning dark hair and the jaws of a bulldog. He held a brown paper bag in one hand and asked to see Leander Thorne.

I didn't move an inch. "Who are you?"

He identified himself as Detective Gary Lipkin, but I didn't take him for his word. I made him show his badge.

"Jon! Let the man in," Leander shouted from inside.

Reluctantly, I escorted Detective Lipkin into the kitchen.

Leander showed no signs of concern or surprise. He smiled as if entertaining cops in the morning was routine to him. "Have a seat, Detective. Coffee?"

Lipkin nodded gratefully. "Black, no sugar."

Leander filled a cup for him, then sat too. Our modest kitchen started to feel crowded. The polite thing would've been to leave them alone. So, I picked up my sketchbook and stayed. I pushed my chair away from the table, but that was all the privacy they'd get.

"I don't think we've met," Leander began.

"You met my nephew, Officer Carter, at the Bowman house."

"Yes, I remember. How's he?"

"Good. Prepping for his Sergeant's exam. You made an impression on him. He says the Bowman boy was exactly where you said. You're supposed to be some kind of psychic."

"And that's why you're here?"

Lipkin's mouth twitched, as if he didn't like what he was about to say. "I want to ask your help finding someone." Without waiting for a reply, he picked the bag off the floor and pulled a gray silk shirt out of it. He placed it on the kitchen table. "This man disappeared three days ago. His wedding's tomorrow."

I noticed dark stains on the front of the shirt—dried blood from the look of it. Leander brushed over them with his fingers. Next he closed his eyes and pressed the fabric to his face. For a minute or two the only sounds in the room were our breathing and the slow drip of the faucet.

At last, Leander opened his eyes. "I have bad news."

"Is he dead?" Lipkin asked, expressionless.

"Worse. Married. And not to his intended bride. He ran off to Vegas with someone else—I think the maid of honor." He plopped the shirt down in front of Lipkin and slumped back in his chair. "But you know this already, Detective, right? Did I pass the test?"

Detective Lipkin's jaws worked, but otherwise his expression remained blank. That poker face must've been a plus in his line of work. "You did all right," he said after a pause. Clearly, the admission took him some effort.

If he was astonished, so was I. Could Leander have genuine psychic skills? Wrapping my head around that notion was a challenge. I decided to withhold judgment just yet. Who knew, maybe Lipkin was a kook.

"What about the blood stains?" I asked.

"Nosebleed," Leander said, rubbing his temples. He kept his eyes on our guest. "So, why are you *really* here, Detective Lipkin?"

The man in question took a slow swig of his coffee. Not being the one asking questions must have been hard on him. "I work in homicide," he started. "I have, for twenty-two years. When you're at it this long you'll have a score of unsolved cases, but there's always one that doesn't leave you alone. Mine happened a bit over nineteen years ago. A young woman was murdered in a motel room in Silverlake. We've never even gotten an ID on her. She was a pretty little thing, hard to imagine nobody missed her."

"And you want me to find out who she was? I've never done anything like that before."

Lipkin shrugged. "This case is colder than a witch's tit. Nobody cares about it but me. So you either come up with a new detail or not. I got nothing to lose."

"Wait a minute," I cut in. "Leander does this for a living. You can't expect a freebie, just because you're a cop."

Lipkin had already given me the once over at the door, but I got a second dose for butting in. I could imagine the cop wheels whirling in his head. Whatever he put together about me and Leander he didn't say. "Mr. Thorne has three outstanding parking tickets, and I have another nephew working in Parking Enforcement. I think we can work something out." I was impressed—he was sly and he'd done his homework.

I looked to Leander for his reaction. He gave me a rueful shrug. "Well, I can try," he said. "Do you have an item of clothing?"

"That's the thing—not a stitch. She was naked and the room was cleared out."

"Then what am I supposed to do?" He threw his hands up.

"We could go to the motel."

"You know how many people must've stayed there in the last twenty years?"

"That's all I got."

Leander sighed. "Fine. Give me the address and I'll meet you there."

Lipkin scribbled the address on a sheet from my sketchbook, and I saw him out. Stepping outside, I pulled the door closed behind me. "Detective."

He raised his brows. "Yes?"

"How close did Leander come?" I gestured at the brown bag.

"Damn close. He was wrong about the maid of honor—the groom ran off with the bride's cousin. He was spot on about Vegas, though."

"Shit."

"You said it." He made an about face and left.

Leander was still in the kitchen, holding my sketchbook, smiling. "You're right, the good detective has a bit of bulldog in him."

A glance at the sheet revealed that while they'd talked, I'd doodled Lipkin with drooping canine jowls. I needed to keep an eye on my hands—they clearly had a mind of their own, and kept getting me in trouble.

He put the pad down. "The dishes are done. I'd better get going."

"I'm going with you."

"I can handle it myself."

"Sure you can. I'm still going. It's better if we take my car. Get your stuff."

He stared at me, pursing his lips, half-amused, half-curious, then said, "Okay, boss."

That was the second time he called me that.

***

Lakeview Motel was a bald-faced lie. The tiny, barred windows hardly provided any view at all, and certainly not of the lake. Room 212 smelled of mold and despair.

"Stay here," Leander gave the order as we stepped inside, so Detective Lipkin and I stuck by the door.

Leander wandered around, touching the walls and the furniture. He leaned back on the bed and remained motionless, while we watched with breathless suspense. He pushed himself up with a frown and toed his shoes off. His socks followed, which he tucked into the shoes. Keeping his eyes closed, he ambled around barefoot. I feared for his toes. He froze at the corner of the bed, spun around, and disappeared into the bathroom.

We found him stretched out in the bathtub, feet under the faucet, head resting on the opposite rim. He didn't move a muscle for several nerve-stretching minutes. I was about to suggest we call it a day when he crossed his arms over his chest so his hands lay around his own neck. He bent his knees and slid down. If there was water in the tub, he would've been submerged.

"Erwin." The way his eyes popped open could've gotten him a scene in a horror flick. I managed not to jump, but with an effort.

Lipkin's shoulders twitched too, and he sucked in air

before asking, "Who's Erwin?"

"He strangled her...Laura...Laurel...not sure." He set up and hugged his knees.

"You sure she was strangled, not drowned?"

I knew Lipkin was testing Leander again since he had to know the answer. Leander stood his ground. "Positive."

It could've been the lighting, but Leander seemed greenish to me. I stepped forward and held my hand in his direction. He took it and climbed out of the tub.

In the other room he sat on the bed to pull his socks and shoes on, but then he froze in mid-motion. "Something's missing. Another person." He gave Lipkin a narrow-eyed glare. "You're holding back."

Lipkin scratched his head. "The night manager told us he saw her take a baby out of the car. But he was a drunk, and we found no trace of a baby, or anything else. The autopsy showed she'd never given birth."

"But you think the manager told the truth, right? Why?"

"Just a hunch."

Leander tied the laces of his red sneakers. "You have crime scene photos?"

"Of course."

"If you get me one, I can try something else. A good picture of her face, if possible."

"Okay."

We said goodbye and climbed into my car. Leander tilted his seat back. "I'm beat. Psyching always wears me out, but this has been the worst ever. Could you drop me off at the park when we're back in Pasadena? I need to recharge."

"I have a better idea," I said and fired up the engine.

***

Griffith Park is a rugged, mountainous place surrounded by urban sprawl. It's much bigger and wilder than Central

Park. Not that I've ever been to the latter, but I bet it doesn't have coyotes and rattlesnakes. I had hiked in Griffith Park many times before, and knew a nice spot off the beaten track. I stopped on a dirt patch between a mulch pile and the bridle trail.

Leander opened his eyes and looked around. "Can you park here?"

"Sure. There's no sign saying otherwise."

"How about that one?" He pointed at the sign thirty feet away as he climbed out.

"That's way over there by the fence. Trust me, we're fine. I've never in my life gotten a parking ticket."

"Oh, rub it in." He stretched and the sun caught in the golden fuzz on his arms.

I looked away. "Are you okay to walk? It's a bit of an uphill."

"I can do it."

I led him up on the dirt path, taking frequent stops under the pretense of admiring the landscape. It was as much for my benefit as his. I hadn't had regular exercise since the accident, and it showed. I made a mental note to look into the gym options at school.

After about fifteen minutes we reached the narrow trail branching out toward a lookout spot. Our trek ended by a couple of permanently wind-bent pine trees. The mundane view of Glendale stretched out below, snuggled under a blanket of smog. A cluster of tallish buildings marked downtown. The rest was a spill of low-rises—apartment buildings of the lowland giving way to single family homes climbing up the hills. Far more impressive, the San Gabriel Mountains towered beyond. The murmur of distant traffic sounded a lot like the ocean, only more even.

"The view's nicer at night," I explained. Darkness and sparkling lights prettied up even the dull suburbs.

Leander laid his hand on one of the trees' rough bark.

"This is nice. How do you know this place?"

"Used to live close by, came here to unwind."

He forged ahead and found a sunny spot to sit. I leaned on the tree and watched him tilt his face toward the sky. "I love the sun. I didn't always." He twisted around to face me. "I wasn't born in California, you know."

"No?" I asked, to encourage him to continue. I had the feeling he needed to talk in order to get his equilibrium back.

"Grams and I moved here from Boston when I was seven. I hated it first. The seasons are fucked up. The ocean is cold. You have to drive everywhere. But most of all I hated the constant sunshine."

"That's crazy talk." I'd grown up in L.A., and the mere idea of long, dark winters filled me with dread.

"The sun here is merciless—always there, sucking everything dry. But I've grown to love it. It's like an immutable, unfeeling God that's always there for you—if you know what I mean."

I didn't. "Not a clue."

He lay back on the ground and laced his fingers together over his chest. The pose reminded me of him in that dingy bathtub, but he seemed livelier now, color returning to his cheeks. "I like to drive to the beach or up to the hills, someplace where I can be alone, and let the sun beat down on me. It feels like I'm part of forever—a tiny speck in time."

"Sounds depressing." I had hard time following—philosophizing had never been my strong suit. This deep thinking stuff unsettled me. I preferred Leander being his usual happy-go-lucky self.

But I'd misjudged the situation. His lips curled into a smile. "No, not at all. It's a relief to be unimportant. I like that about California—it's easy to get lost here."

"Ain't that the truth," I agreed with relief.

He craned his neck and squinted at me. "Jon, can I ask you

something?"

"Shoot."

"How did your wife die?"

He couldn't have shocked me more if he'd punched me in the gut. I had no words.

"You're wearing a wedding ring, but you live alone, not counting me. If you were divorced, you would've taken it off. It could've been a guy, but my gut says it wasn't," he explained when I stayed mute.

"Oh." I looked down at the yellow band around my finger. It had been there so long, I wasn't even aware of it anymore.

"You don't have to tell me if you don't want."

It made no difference if I did or not, the facts were facts. Also, after having witnessed his...thing in the motel, I felt I owed him a scrap of honesty. "Alicia and I were coming back from a Thanksgiving Day visit to her family in Palmdale. She drove because I'd had a couple of beers. Traffic was backed up on the freeway, so we took the scenic route. She lost control of the car. I grabbed for the wheel, but we rolled. She died, I didn't." I left out the part that it had been the first time in years she'd seen her mother and it had upset her, like I'd known it would.

I'd listened to that crackpot shrink of hers, who'd kept yammering on about how Alicia needed to reconnect with her family in order to overcome the past and heal. Bullshit. What she'd needed was to stay the hell away from the whole toxic bunch, and I should've made sure she did. At least I shouldn't have had those beers with her idiot brother, and I should've been behind the wheel. I couldn't think of that day without a stab of regret, but I only thought of it three, maybe four times a day by now.

"And you've been blaming yourself for the accident ever since."

"You're going to tell me I shouldn't." Others had. *It wasn't your fault*, was easy for them to say, but it'd been my job to keep her safe, always.

Leander slowly shook his head. "I could, but it wouldn't make any difference. Did you love her?"

"With all my heart. From the moment we met in first grade." If I closed my eyes, I could still recall her shy smile and lopsided pigtails. "Love is a strange beast."

"And you're an unusual man." The tenderness in his gaze bored under my skin leaving a dull ache. Thank God, he tipped his face skyward. "Come, lie down next to me and feel the sun."

"The ground must be crawling with ants."

"Don't be a wuss."

How could I refuse such a challenge? I stepped forward, sat on a patch of dry grass and leaned back. Rocks dug into my ribs and dry pine needles poked my scalp. I closed my eyes, and let the sun beat down on me. After a while some of the heaviness lifted as I let myself be insignificant. Leander shifted so our shoulders touched. There was an unexpected comfort in it.

***

A photo arrived from Lipkin the following week. Leander sat in the kitchen glaring at it one day as I arrived home for lunch.

"How's it going?" I asked, popping a Tupperware container in the microwave.

He frowned. "Not good. I'm not getting anything."

"Maybe it's for the best."

He slid the picture into its envelope. "You're probably right. I'd rather search for lost pets. That reminds me—I need to go find a Chihuahua in Runyon Canyon." He stood and slung his bag over his shoulder.

"What happened?" I asked.

"The owner let it off the leash."

"Dumb move." Runyon Canyon was a popular park and

hiking place in the hills above Hollywood. You could spot semi-celebrities there. Like Griffith Park, it also had its share of wildlife, including coyotes. "The odds are against you."

He sighed. "I know. I'd better ask for payment up front."

"And put on sunscreen."

He went still, and looked at me as if I said something amusing.

"You burn easily," I explained.

He shook his head, but I caught a glimpse of a smile before he turned away. "See you tonight."

He left, and I ate my lunch before heading back to campus. After the drawing class I stayed in the studio to work on a larger piece. When I got home, I found him in the living room, sitting sideways in an armchair, reading. He lifted his head to give me a quick greeting.

"Success?" I asked.

He made a face. "We found Caesar's collar."

"*Caesar*? Didn't you say it was a Chihuahua?"

"Yup. Apparently, the owner is an actress. She's on that soap, you know, the one set in a hospital."

I shrugged. "I wouldn't know."

"Well, her name's Myra Banks, and she's destined for greatness. According to her, anyway. Have you ever heard of her?"

"Nope."

"Me neither, before today. I dunno, she seemed so fake. Like she acted frantic about the dog, but still managed to tell me all about her role on the show, and the directors she wanted to work with, and so on. It was hard to concentrate with her constantly jabbering."

"Well, let's hope she doesn't move from dogs to having kids. Coyotes are not picky."

His eyes opened wide in horror.

***

Dreams will set you free or trap you. I preferred not having them at all. What I hated most, was being shaken awake from a blissfully dreamless sleep. I bolted straight up with my heart racing. "What's wrong?"

A splash of light from the window made Leander's face glow against the gloom of the room. "I had a strange dream," he said.

I flopped back on the bed, rubbing my face. "Jesus Christ. I thought the house was on fire. What time is it?"

"Five a.m. Sorry."

I checked the alarm clock for confirmation. It was indeed the crack of dawn. "You're up at this hour? Why?"

"I told you, I had a dream."

"That happens when you sleep."

"This was different, very vivid. I was in a car, except, I wasn't me, but the murdered girl, and she, I mean I, was alive. Erwin and I were driving through a forest in a storm. The rain beating down the roof of the car sounded like drumming. I could barely see through the windows. Then out of nowhere this huge, black bird smashed into the windshield. Scared the hell out of me. And that's when I woke up."

"Fascinating. You should tell Detective Lipkin about it," I snarked.

"I already did," he said innocently.

"What? You called him at this hour? Are you out of your freaking mind?"

"Funny, he used the exact same words. He also said to tell you about it, right away."

"Fucking bastard. I'll sue him for police brutality."

"He had a good point. I could see Erwin's face as clear as I can see you. You could draw him for me before I forget. Like police sketch artists do."

His hopeful expression caused a dull ache in my chest that

I didn't need, but I couldn't look away. "I'm not that good."

He didn't believe me. "You'll do better than I would. I can only draw stick figures."

What the hell could I say? I wouldn't be able to go back to sleep anyhow. "Fine. But I want coffee first."

It took us a good while to commit "Erwin's" face to paper. Leander and I sat shoulder-to-shoulder on the sofa working on it. He kept poking his finger at my sketch, giving directions, while I, with pencil and eraser in hand, tried to follow them. To my alarm, we worked well together. Erwin turned out to be a handsome fellow with a small mole on his chin.

"That's perfect. You rock!" Leander said with enthusiasm. He gave me a sideways hug and a kiss on the cheek. I hated how good it felt.

I extracted myself from his arms and stood. "I'll fix breakfast." There was no point in going back to bed by then.

Detective Lipkin must've felt the same, because he arrived in time for the next pot of coffee.

He held the sketch out at arm's length. "So this is our guy?"

"The way I saw him. Isn't Jon just so talented?" Leander gushed.

I shook my head at him. "You realize that's him probably twenty years ago? As seen in a dream."

Lipkin shrugged. "This is the best lead I've gotten in two decades." He fixed his gaze on Leander. "You said it was raining."

Leander nodded. "Cats and dogs."

"And the bird flew into the windshield."

"Yes, I told you already."

"What color was the car?"

Leander squinted. "I dunno, dark. I think."

Lipkin slid the sketch into the envelope I'd given him

earlier. "I haven't told you, but the night manager reported seeing a blue Ford Thunderbird."

"Thunder and bird? Are you saying my dreams are talking to me in code?"

"Don't ask me. You're the psychic."

"Right. I'm off to shower," I announced and left them alone.

When I returned, clean and ready for school, Leander sat at the table by himself, still in his pajamas, hair tousled, Thomas Guide and other maps laid out in front of him. Eyes shut, he bent over them and slowly traced a finger on the paper. He stopped, opened his eyes and made a mark on the map. I watched from the door as he pulled out another one and started the process over.

"What are you up to?" I asked when he put pen to paper again.

"Tracing." He laid the two maps next to each other. "I got the idea of starting from the Lakeview Motel to see if I got anywhere."

"And you did." I walked up behind him and took a peek over his shoulder. The spots matched almost exactly, indicating a location in the western part of Angeles National Forest. I knew the area—good camping and fishing in that region.

"There's something there," he said.

I leaned closer. "Canyons and lakes country. I'll tell you what—I don't have afternoon classes today. We can take a ride out there."

The way I figured, he'd go anyway, in that rickety car of his. If he broke down, he'd call me and I'd end up having to go rescue him. If he could get cell phone reception out there at all, that was. He could end up having to ask a stranger for help, and the idea of that didn't sit well with me. I'd save us both time and trouble by driving.

He beamed. "That would be great. Thank you."

"Don't mention it. I better shove off to class. See you noon-ish."

"Perfect. I have time to go to the hardware store."

"What for?"

"A shovel, of course."

Oh, hell.

***

We set off after lunch. Leander had crammed a backpack full of food, water, sweaters, sunscreen, and God knows what else.

"We're not camping," I pointed out.

He frowned and cast his gaze around the room. No doubt trying to decide what else to stuff into the bag. "You never know what'll come in handy. I know I'm forgetting something."

"The kitchen sink?"

He pursed his lips. "You're very funny. Okay, let's go."

The traffic was light by L.A. standards, and we were making good time. It was a nice day, warm but not hot, with a light breeze—perfect for a road trip.

Leander pushed his seat back and put his feet on the dashboard. I was going to yell at him for it at first, but the sight of his cheery red canvas sneakers changed my mind.

"I've never been camping in my life. It seemed so awfully romantic when I was a kid," he said.

"I don't know about romantic, but it's relaxing."

"Grams and I went on day trips, but she liked to sleep in her own bed, and have hot and cold running water in the morning. The closest I ever got was a sleepover with another kid. We spent the night in a tent in his backyard."

"Alicia and I used to—" Her name slipped out but I caught myself. I remembered the discomfort on my friends' faces when I'd brought her up.

I felt Leander's searching gaze on me. "You can talk about her to me."

Right, he'd never met her. Maybe that made a difference. "She and I went camping whenever we could. We both enjoyed getting away from the city for a couple of days. We'd laze around, talk, swim and make S'mores in the evening." They were some of the best times we had together.

"If you don't mind me asking, why did you two get married?"

Did I mind? Probably, but could at least give him the short version. "Because she was my best friend, and I wanted to get her away from that pack of hyenas that was her family, and make sure nobody hurt her." Again.

He didn't respond, and we kept to small talk for the rest of the trip, but I caught him scrutinizing me a few times.

I took an exit not far past Santa Clarita and soon we were surrounded by nature. The parched hills and canyons wore colors from pale yellow to rust. Only the trees along a creek bed flaunted bright green. A Smokey the Bear sign at the side of the road warned us of a very high fire danger.

Southern California has only three true seasons—summer, fire and wet. We had only a few months when it rained at all. While most of the country slept under snow, our hillsides flourished. But the long summer had leached every last bit of moisture from the land. By now we were deep into fire season—if you just looked at a clump of shrubbery the wrong way, it would burst into flames.

I drove nice and slow as it was more relaxing, but also because the two-lane road was edged by steep drops but no guardrails. After about forty-five minutes of this, Leander perked up like a dog on the scent.

"Slow down," he said as we neared a bend in the road.

We crept along for another couple of minutes.

"Turn there." He pointed at a campground sign up ahead.

I did so and under his instructions drove all the way to the far end. The smallish campsite hid among tall trees and a tiny stream ran through it. It was a nice spot for camping, but at the moment we were the only two people there. Leander climbed out of the car, taking the backpack with him. He stood motionless for a moment, sniffing the air, then headed down a trail. I locked the car and followed. About fifty feet down he veered off into the underbrush.

"Here somewhere." He tromped around, frustrated. Finally, he sat on a log and took his shoes and socks off.

"You're gonna hurt your feet," I warned him.

"Can't be helped." He shuffled around among the trees.

With nothing better to do, I kept watching till he came to a stop.

"This is it, I think," he said. He dropped the bag, took a couple of gardening trowels out, and handed one of them to me. "We dig."

"With these?"

"They only had very big shovels at the hardwood store. And these."

"Shoulda gone to a sports store. They have camping supplies."

"Oh. Well, too late now."

He knelt and dug into the soil, and I followed suit. We shoveled dirt in silence till the tip of my trowel hit something hard. After clearing away more dirt I knew for sure it wasn't a rock. The bone stood out smooth and pale-white against the dark earth. My heart started to beat faster. We could've found the remains of a mule deer, but I knew we didn't. I was no expert, but judging from its size, we'd dug up a human thighbone.

"Well fuck," I said. The fun had gone out of this road trip for good.

Leander, who had stopped digging and only watched, let out a deep sigh. "I was afraid of this."

"Did you have another dream?"

"No, but I had a bad feeling."

I knew how that felt. "We should've let Lipkin know about coming here."

"I didn't know. I've never done anything like this before." He reached out and touched the bare bone with the tips of his fingers. After a minute of silence, he pulled his hand back and rubbed it on his jeans. "It's a woman. Young."

"How can you be sure?"

"I felt it." He stood and hobbled back to the log.

I walked after him. "You hurt your feet didn't you?"

"It's nothing."

"Let me see."

He sat, and I inspected the sole of his feet. "A small cut, but it's covered in dirt—could get infected. I bet you don't have a first aid kit in that bag."

"See, I told you I'd forgotten something."

"Lucky for you, I have one in the trunk. C'mon."

I looped an arm around his waist and we made it back to the car. He sat sideways on the front seat while I got the kit. Checking my phone I saw it had two measly bars. Lucky we had any reception at all.

I handed it to Leander. "Call Lipkin."

While he did, I got on my knees, cleaned out the cut, put antibacterial ointment on it and a bandage. "There you are. Be careful putting weight on it. What did Lipkin say?" I asked straightening up.

"He's on his way, and will get here when he gets here. Meanwhile we need to call the regular police. Oh yeah, and we should keep the psychic stuff under our hats."

I called 911, even though it was no emergency—they would let the local police know. I knew it would take the cops some time to get there. We were in a national park about halfway between Santa Clarita and Lancaster. The dead woman had been that way for a long time. Half an hour here or there made no difference to her.

Leander and I wandered over to a large tree trunk lying in the middle of the campsite. I leaned on it, and he swung a leg across. Around us wind rustled the leaves, insects buzzed, and death lurked in the underbrush.

"It's strange," Leander said with a pensive shadow over his face.

"What is?"

"There's a murdered girl right over there, yet it's so peaceful."

I hummed in agreement. People who died of natural causes rarely ended up in shallow graves in the woods. And it was peaceful. Nicer than any cemetery I've been to.

Heaviness sat on my chest and it was going to suffocate me if I didn't throw it off. "I haven't told you the truth."

Leander cocked his head. "About what?"

"Alicia. I didn't lie, but there's more to the story. She and I were meant to be together. I knew I'd marry her when we were six, the day we met."

"So you like women too?" Curiosity rang in his voice, but not judgment.

"Not that way, but not everything comes down to sex. We both had phenomenally fucked up families. My parents hated each other with an epic passion, and the only thing they ever agreed on was what a disappointment I was. Hers…yeah well, let's not even go there. If we hadn't had each other growing up, I don't think either of us would've made it into adulthood. She was my only true family, and I was hers. We didn't have a conventional marriage, but so what? We still did better than many couples I know."

"I suspect conventional relationships are a fiction. The reality's always a bit screwy."

"I think most of our friends thought of me as her caretaker. Alicia had lupus and had flare-ups. She also suffered from emotional problems, bouts of depression. On the surface she looked fragile, but she had inner strength. She was the first person I told about being gay, and she didn't bat an eye. Whenever I started to think of myself as abnormal, a freak, she set me straight. Still, sometime it was hard. Even when you love somebody…" I didn't know how to finish that sentence. Everything about her, me, the two of us together was complicated.

Leander took my hand and squeezed. "Grams got sick. Towards the end she needed constant care. When she died I felt grief, but also a relief. It was terrible."

A choked sound escaped my throat. He understood. Nothing more needed to be said.

The hushed noises of the forest wrapped around us. I stared off to the direction of the dirt trail. "I wonder how she got lost."

"People do ugly things to each other. That body would've stayed there who knows how long, if we hadn't found it. Makes you wonder how many others are out there, unfound. When you watch those TV shows, they only tell you about cases that got solved. I bet there are many more that didn't."

"Not something I like to ponder." The question on my mind was whether Erwin killed this girl too, and if he was some kind of serial killer. Could he be still out there, killing women? And most importantly, could we stop him? I caught myself. All I did was drive. Leander did the heavy lifting. I took his hand, still lying on mine and kneaded his fingers. "I didn't always believe you. The psychic stuff, I mean."

"I know. You told me I wasn't real. It's okay. Skepticism is healthy."

"How do you do it? Explain it to me."

He scratched his head. "Well, with lost cats and dogs a favorite toy lets me tune in to them. It's a lot like meditation—I empty my mind and let them fill it. After that I can trace them on the map."

"How exactly does that work?"

"It's very simple. I start where they disappeared from and feel the right track in my fingertip. People are harder, the emotions are more complex. Like in the Lakeview Motel…" He grimaced.

"Yes?"

"It was like I slipped inside Erwin. I felt what he felt, while he strangled that girl. Strange though, it was more grief than anger."

"Odd."

"Emotion is the key to making a connection. Love, hate, desire, sorrow. The stronger the better."

"Right," I said, but I still didn't really understand.

"They tested me when I was thirteen. There was this man in white lab coat who had cards with geometric shapes on them, and I was supposed to guess which one he was looking at. Scientific method, right? I so flunked. But you know, it's hard to get worked up about geometric shapes."

"I can see that." They'd never done anything for me either.

He dug the toe of one of his sneakers into the dirt. "Science disregards emotions because they can't be measured." He hesitated for a moment, but went on. "You know about Apollo 13, right?"

Of course I did, I wasn't dumb. "I saw the movie with Tom Hanks."

"Then you know what slim chance the astronauts had of making it back to Earth alive. Sure, all that smart stuff they did—and ground control too—they were real, but it still could've gone horribly wrong. Right?"

"Well, yes, I guess."

"I have a theory there was another element in play."

"Emotions?" I asked incredulously.

"Millions of people around the world looking up the sky and willing them to return safe. It had to be like this giant, invisible beam of power to guide the ship to Earth," he said with a shy smile.

Sounded like a pretty far-fetched idea to me, but I got the impression it was a secret he'd shared with me. "I think you're a fruit," I said, warmly.

He winked. "You bet. More ways than one."

I shook my head in fake exasperation. He shifted his backside and leaned into me. I let him.

"What are we going to tell the cops? They'll wonder how we just happened on a dead body in the middle of nowhere," he said.

I had an idea, not great, but plausible enough.

***

A park ranger arrived first. Surveying the bone, he made *hm* sounds and radioed his supervisor. The second ranger took a look too, and his already serious expression got even more so. The first black-and-white showed up a good forty-five minutes after our phone call, but the campsite filled with official vehicles pretty fast after that.

The cops separated Leander and me right away, but I'd warned him about that already. I found myself answering the same questions over and over, and I supposed Leander did the same. We'd agreed to give making a cat hole as a reason for digging. A cat hole is something many campers and hikers use when they have to take a shit in the woods. Not an unreasonable explanation, we just had to stick to our guns. I'd stressed that part to Leander. For the rest we told the truth—it's always the easiest thing to keep straight. The cops treated us with suspicion, but that was their job. We had a few things in our favor—the bones had obviously been in the ground for some time, and we called the police when we could've easily driven away. After repeating my story a few times, they deposited me in the back of one of the patrol cars, but without handcuffs.

At long last, Detective Lipkin arrived too and pulled the lead cop aside. They had a long conversation, but in the end Leander and I were let go. Lipkin gave us an earful about not getting him in the loop before going corpse-hunting, then told us to get lost and keep our noses clean.

We left but pulled over before getting to the freeway and ate the sandwiches Leander had packed. We were starving. He offered to drive, but I declined.

"The accident, didn't it make you nervous about driving?" he asked.

"About driving? No. Being a passenger, yes."

He nodded. "You trust yourself, but not others. Makes sense."

That was one way of putting it.

Chapter Four

A few days later we got a call from Lipkin, letting us know he hadn't had an official word from the coroner's office yet. However, he'd had unofficial confirmation the body had been in the ground for years, possibly decades, and it was female. He didn't divulge anything else, and we didn't hear from him again for weeks.

Leander and I went about our lives. I had midterms coming up and prepping for them kept me busy. The art classes were easiest because there were no exams, just more drawing. My English professor wanted us to write a research essay but without using the Internet to look up stuff. So I spent a lot of time in the library.

Art History was the hardest, but fortunately I was taking the class for pass or fail. I liked it okay, but I'm shit for remembering names and dates. To make things worse, it was my third class on Tuesdays, from six to nine at night. Whenever we had a slide show, I had to fight to keep my eyes open in the dark. I sat at the back of the class and asked the girl next to me to poke me if I dozed off.

At night I started to have dreams in which I forgot to go to an exam, or showed up, only to realize I wasn't wearing pants. I slept fitfully and waking up in the middle of the night was normal for me. However, finding a ghost in stripy pajamas sitting on the edge of my bed was definitely not normal.

It took my foggy brain long seconds to process the scene and determine I wasn't seeing a ghost.

"Jon, are you awake?" Leander asked.

I bit back a curse. "Am now. What the hell are you doing here?"

"I was watching you sleep," he replied matter-of-factly.

I rubbed my eyes. "Why?" I knew I would regret asking, even as the word left my lips.

He shrugged. He also pulled his feet up, making himself entirely too comfortable on *my* bed.

"You can't just waltz in here whenever you feel like it." A suspicious thought invaded my mind. "Hey, have you done it before?"

"First time, I swear." He took a deep breath, held it, and let it out in a big whoosh. "I had a fucked-up dream."

No. I wasn't going there. I wasn't his...anything. "How old are you?"

"Twenty-two. I've told you. Why?"

"Old enough to deal with your own nightmares. Or buy a nightlight."

Two parallel lines appeared between his brows. "It wasn't a nightmare. Not really. That girl we found—Erwin didn't kill her."

Curiosity got the best of me. "Then who did?"

"Laura."

"The other dead girl from the motel?"

"Yup. She strangled this girl. In the dream I felt both of them, but there was too much anger and jealousy. I woke up, thank God, and didn't want to go back to sleep."

"And came to watch me?"

"You snore, you know."

"I've been told."

"I like it. Grams snored too—I find it comforting."

I didn't have the energy to be pissed at him any longer. "You're a fruit and a half. Go back to bed." I rolled to my other side and pulled the blanket up to my chin, hoping he'd get the message.

There was a rustle, and the next I knew, naked flesh pressed against my back.

"What the hell are you doing?" I protested, rolling over.

He used it as an opportunity to slip farther down, tugging

at the waistband of my boxers as he went. I should've stopped him and kicked him out of bed, but I was only made of flesh. Neglected, needy flesh. The warm, wet suction of his mouth had me hard before I could say *holy fuck*. I had to give him this—he knew what he was doing. He had the face of innocence, but the tongue of sin. What really got to me though, was the tenderness of it. You'd think it's all the same—friction, saliva, heat—but you can tell when someone's doing it with feeling. It's a subtle difference, measurable only by nerve endings, and the shadow of guilt you feel when you know you can't return it in kind. For a crazy moment I thought maybe I could, but my charred heart said no—too risky.

So I emptied my mind and forced my focus onto the physical sensations. With Leander's skilled fingers caressing my balls, and his lips and throat around my cock, I didn't last very long.

Not reciprocating would've been plain rude, so once I got my breathing back to normal, I flipped him on his back, and proceeded to return the blow job. I gave it my best. I let him dig his fingers into my hair, but not to take charge.

Something got into me, because instead of getting him off quickly, I drew out the proceedings. Maybe I wanted to show off. Maybe I enjoyed the frustrated noises he made when I brought him to the brink and eased off. He let out a few remarkably filthy curses. I would've laughed if it wasn't impossible with his cock down my throat.

I hoped he'd go back to his own bed once we were done, but he stretched out on mine and fell asleep almost immediately. The heat of another body next to mine, the sound of breathing—they were scarily familiar and comforting. It would've been so easy to wrap myself around him, but instincts of self-preservation stopped me. Shifting to the other side of the bed I pulled a pillow over my head. It took me a long while to find a measure of peace and fall asleep.

We didn't talk about it the next day or after, and it didn't happen again. I told myself it was for the best, and that the gnawing emptiness inside me was perfectly normal.

***

Detective Lipkin showed up unannounced one evening, a few days after my finals. He appeared tired and worse for wear, but as bulldoggish as ever. I offered him a seat in the living room, which he took. "You probably want to know what the investigation uncovered," he started.

We nodded. I was mildly curious, but Leander had been on pins and needles since that last call, I could tell.

Lipkin took a notepad and a pair of reading glasses out of his breast pocket. He put the glasses on. "Have you ever seen that TV show about what would happen if people disappeared from the face of the earth? I have. It's fascinating. Buildings, roads, they'll turn to dust in no time. Everything but plastic."

"Uh-huh." I wondered where he was going with this.

He flipped the pad open. "When the forensic technicians dug up that body, they found a laminated library card among the remains. Everything else, except the bones, rotted away, but the plastic held up. The card was made out to a Megan Forest of Fulton, Idaho."

Leander leaned forward, eyes like blue lasers focused on Lipkin. "That's some break. What did you find in Fulton?"

"Quite a lot, actually." The detective glanced at his notes. "Megan Forest was born in Pocatello, Idaho, into a big family. Four boys, two girls—her and her older sister, Lauren."

Leander slapped his forehead. "Duh! Lauren."

Lipkin shot a reproachful glare at Leander over the frame of his glasses.

"Go on," Leander said.

"Lauren married a man named Erwin Harris, as soon as

she reached legal age. Erwin was a handyman and fourteen years her senior. Her parents didn't care for the match, but as I came to understand, she was the black sheep of the family. The newlyweds moved to Fulton. A couple of years later when Megan, the younger sister, turned eighteen, she joined them too. Apparently, she wasn't getting along with her parents either. The girls became estranged from the family at this point, but didn't seem to mind. I talked to their neighbors, many of whom still remembered them. Fulton's a small town, and the trio made a big impression." He glanced at me. "By the way, the people I talked to said your drawing of Erwin was spot on."

"Jon's awesome," Leander gushed. I kept my mouth shut.

Lipkin gave him another glare of reprimand. "As I was saying, Erwin and the girls, but especially the girls, made an impression. They had a stormy relationship, best friends in one minute, fighting like wild cats the next. When young Megan got pregnant, it became the talk of the town. Everyone believed Erwin to be the father. Sure enough, the birth certificate for Evelyn Forest stated so. A few months after the baby's birth the four of them were on the move again. Lauren told one of the neighbors they were moving to California. She also hinted that they could make good money by letting some rich California folks adopt baby Evelyn." He flipped his notes closed.

"So what happened next?" Leander asked impatiently.

"I don't think we'll ever know. Somewhere along the way Megan ended up dead, and they buried her body where you found it. Lauren took over her sister's role, and they completed the adoption. If they made money on it, Erwin got to keep it. Maybe that was his plan all along, and that's why he killed Megan."

Leander shook his head. "No. He didn't kill her. It was Lauren."

Lipkin raised his eyebrows in surprise, but then he shrugged. "If you say so. At any rate, he killed Lauren and went on like nothing happened, didn't even change his name or try to disappear."

"You found him?" Leander's voice shot up an octave.

"So to speak. He died two years ago. But I located his widow—yes, he remarried. She told me when she'd gone through Erwin's stuff after his death, she'd found adoption papers among them. It shocked her, because Erwin had told her he hadn't had children."

Leander deflated. "That blows."

"She also found this." Lipkin took a Polaroid out of his pocket and held it out.

Leander took it, and I leaned closer to take a peek. Two young women smiled into the camera, holding a bundle between them. Wind ruffled their blond hair. A patch of blue and green showed in the background. The photo's original colors had faded and shifted with time, and its focus was fuzzy.

Leander stared at it for a long time before handing it back. "What's going to happen now?"

"Now? Nothing. It would take a court order to unseal the adoption records, and that won't happen. There's no cause for it."

"But Evelyn, she should know—"

"Know what? That her father was a murderer, or that he buried her mother in the woods? No person needs to know that."

Leander sank into a sour-faced sulk and I saw Detective Lipkin out myself. I followed him out to the hallway, as I wanted to have a word. "Leander doesn't normally do this sort of stuff. His specialty is finding lost pets," I told him.

"Yes. So?"

"It was hard on him, he's too young for this shit. So feel free to be a stranger in the future."

We exchanged hard glares, before he walked away without

a goodbye.

In the apartment Leander still sat where I'd left him, cheery as a storm cloud.

"This has all been pointless," he said.

I shrugged and parked my ass on the sofa. "That's life. Shit happens, and the world goes on, with or without you."

He didn't appreciate my worldview. "Well, aren't you a ray of sunshine?" he snapped.

"Relax. Let's watch TV."

He snatched the remote out of my hand and threw it across the room, where it landed with a loud clatter. "I don't want to watch the fucking TV. Don't you get it? Two people were murdered, and got no justice. A baby disappeared and she's still gone. It's not how it's supposed to be. I need some fucking closure or I'll explode! I had dead people in my head for what? This is bullshit!"

I would've never pegged him for one with a temper, but there it was. The funny thing was, I didn't mind. I liked him taking a stand, even if he was in the wrong in this case. Not to mention, flared nostrils and glowering eyes made him unexpectedly attractive.

I kept my voice calm and smooth as velvet. "*Andy*, relax. You're looking at it the wrong way. Detective Lipkin got his closure. He can lay this case to rest and won't spend his retirement years thinking up nightmare scenarios about what might have happened to that baby. And the kid's out there somewhere living a perfectly average life, like many other adopted children. So, in the end, it's better now, thanks to you."

He wrapped himself into a stubborn silence, so I picked up a magazine and let him stew. I lowered it when he exhaled loudly.

"You're right. I didn't think of it that way," he said.

"Of course not. And by the way, if the remote's broken, you're buying a new one."

He stood and walked across the room to where the plastic pieces lay and brought them back. The lid had popped off and the batteries had fallen out, but the rest was in one piece. After reassembling them he pointed it at the set pushed the power button. It worked. *Cupcake Wars* was on.

We watched it for a few seconds before he muted it and gave me a searching look. "Tell me something, and don't lie. You said you didn't want to get involved. Why?"

That was easy. "Because I don't want to have anything it would hurt to lose." There. He could take it or leave it.

He pursed his lips. "You know, you called me Andy."

That took me aback, but I hid it. "I did? So what?"

"You always call me by my full name. Andy is a nickname. Which you just gave me."

"So it is. Don't make a big deal of it."

"Don't worry, I won't."

From the flicker of his eyelashes I knew he was lying.

DEAD IN THE VALLEY

Chapter One

December charged into town riding hot Santa Ana winds. I'd felt it in my bad shoulder the morning before, and it had tickled whatever sixth sense Andy had.

"*Something wicked this way comes*," he'd chanted over breakfast.

"That's Harry Potter, right?" I'd asked.

"Yeah, and Shakespeare."

"Smart-ass."

By that evening the wind picked up, and I went to sleep to the sound of it battering the street signs outside. I woke up in a strange mood and a strange bed. I had to have wandered into Leander's room during the night. Talk about embarrassing. At least I was alone. I couldn't remember a shred of my dream but residual emotions were churning through me, leaving me off-kilter.

Andy walked in just as I was about to get up. "Coffee?" He held the mug out as if finding me in his bed was the most natural thing in the world.

I took it and took a cautious sip before saying anything. "I'm sorry about..." I didn't know exactly what, beyond the invasion of his bed.

"No worries, you were sleepwalking again."

Again? "You knew?"

"Well, I've had a suspicion for some time now, but when you climbed into my bed last night, I was sure you weren't your normal wakeful self." He rolled his eyes.

"What did I do?"

"Tucked in and fell asleep. No biggie." With a shrug he turned away.

I slowly drank the rest of my coffee as he puttered around the room. He was barefoot and shirtless, and his jeans hung low on his narrow hips, showing off the two round dips on his lower back.

The past month or so hadn't been easy on me. Ever since we agreed to be friends, Andy kept worming his way into my life. I had a set schedule built around my classes, while he was freewheeling as a psychic locator of pets and other lost property. Somehow he still managed to be home the same time as I was. Soon I was feeding him three times a day, except on Fridays when I had only half an hour for lunch. In exchange he offered to do the grocery shopping. It was a logical arrangement, but made our situation all the more disturbingly domestic. He was like a puppy, always underfoot, but too playful to get angry with him.

Briefly I tried to think of him as a younger brother but stopped. It creeped me out. The unbidden thoughts darting through my mind in his presence were far from brotherly. He was hot as hell in that young and lithe way I'd never cared much for before. Apparently, my tastes had changed with age. I knew my reasons for keeping my paws off him were solid and smart, and my resolve had held. However, this morning I didn't feel quite like myself.

Over the rim of my cup I spied him folding laundry. With his back to me, he knelt in front a plastic basket, arranging the folded pieces in haphazard piles around himself—boxers, T-shirts, jeans. He rolled socks in tight balls. I eyed his milky skin stretching over wiry muscles and the soft bumps of his spine. Desire sat, heavy as lead, in the pit of my soul. I wanted to jump out of bed and touch. It took some effort to stay put.

Andy picked up the stack of shirts and carried it to the dresser. As he walked by me, a scent of citrus grazed my senses. When he passed again, I reached out and grabbed his wrist with my free hand. I did it without thinking, but once we made contact I was committed to following through.

He registered a mild surprise. "Hey." He tugged at his hand, but I held it firm.

I plunked the cup on the night table and got hold of his hip, pulling him to me.

"Now, wait a minute," he protested, but I paid no heed.

His objections died off as I tumbled him into the bed and covered his lips with mine. When I peeled him out of his jeans I had hard evidence he didn't mind my advances at all.

For once, I didn't hurry. I took my time to taste Andy's skin, trace the hills and valleys of his body, like I'd seen him trace maps. There are so many different textures to human skin, from the rough ridges of nipples to the soft patch behind the knees. And then my favorite, the coarse-haired warm jungle of the groin. While I did my exploring there, Andy was limited to the bumps on the top of my head. Less when I turned him over. He gave out a burbling laugh as I rubbed my stubbled chin down along his spine, and gasped when I bit his left buttock—not too hard.

He joggled his hip. "The other one too, or I'll be asymmetrical."

I complied, before pulling him up to his knees. He began to moan softly at first, then louder as my tongue ventured into the canyon between his cheeks.

"I love your tongue," he managed to say at one point.

Ready to travel deeper, I straightened up and rubbed my cock between his buttocks. He groaned.

"Condoms?" I asked.

He flailed an arm in the direction of the nightstand. "Drawer."

I found everything I needed there. Even with the generous use of lube, he felt so very tight, and I pushed in slowly. The sounds Andy made came dangerously close to whimpers. However when I paused, he pushed back against me, urging me to go on. He was sweetly responsive, reacting to every touch, every change of pace like an old lover who knew my quirks. A worrying thought, but it couldn't get to me, not then. I wrapped myself around him, burying myself into the scent of citrus and the tight heat of his body. Only when I felt the familiar tingle of impending release did I pull him up on his knees, so I could pound into him harder. He came with my hand on his cock, fists gripping the comforter, and moaning loudly. I'd been holding back, but couldn't have waited any longer even if I wanted to.

Silence. It's never completely quiet in the city. There's traffic, planes, helicopters, but you get used to them the same way country people get used to the buzz of insects. This morning seemed more hushed than usual. I stared at the ceiling as the post-coital peace ebbed away, letting the usual worries creep back in. They were in a pique, wanting to know what the hell had possessed me. Instead of trying to come up with an explanation, I tilted my head toward the motion to my right.

Andy rolled on his side, propped his head on his elbow, and gave me a squinty look. "You're doing it already."

"Doing what?"

"Pulling away. Any second now you'll swear never to do this again. It's totally annoying, you know."

I rubbed my face. He had a point: it was time to cut my own bullshit. "All right, Andy, what do you want?"

"A good bonking more than once a month would be nice to start. I swear, you have more sexual hang-ups than a nun."

"I don't have sexual hang-ups!"

"Right, right. You have relationship hang-ups. I still can't see why we couldn't be friends with benefits. Just two guys, no strings attached. Other people do it."

It sounded so simple when he said it. "Okay." I knew it

was a bad idea, but reckless optimism took over me.

"Okay?" He asked with confusion. He'd probably expected more resistance.

"That's what I said, didn't I?"

He grinned like an idiot and then leaned in and bit my jaw.

"Hey! Stop that or I'll have to muzzle you."

"Stop crying. It wasn't hard." He rolled out of bed and yanked his briefs on.

"What time is it? I must be late for school."

"I don't think there's school today. The electricity is out and there are trees blocking streets all over Pasadena. I heard it on the radio. And by the way, I took the spare batteries from the earthquake kit you have in the hallway closet. I've never known anyone with an actual earthquake kit before. It's totally you. Always prepared."

"Whoa, whoa, slow down. What's with the trees?"

"The wind. It knocked them down. It's a complete arboreal massacre out there. You can see one of the causalties from the window."

I rolled out of the bed and looked. Indeed there it was—a large tree down the street splayed across the road. Our building sat on a side street, on which not a single car moved right now. Something must've been blocking the road in the other direction too.

***

A quick call to school confirmed that morning classes were definitely cancelled. I took a lukewarm shower, shaved, and put on a sweater. The apartment was getting cooler. The heat was gas, but without the electric thermostat turning it on, it was useless. Well, at least the stove worked, and we had cooked breakfast.

"Wanna go for a walk?" Andy asked.

I'd been trying to decide what to do with my unexpected free time, so I agreed.

I was surprised to see Andy pulling on gloves. Even for December, we were in L.A. The sun shone as brightly as ever, and by noon the temperature would be in the sixties. A sweater and a jacket sufficed. But Andy was Andy.

We started to wander around aimlessly. The destruction was much worse than I'd imagined. The wind had knocked around anything light enough and not tied down. At one of the gas stations the roof over the pumps had collapsed. The trees had done the most damage though, crashing on cars, roofs, and roads. They seemed too massive to topple over so easily—after all the wind hadn't tossed cars around—but their canopies were big as sails and their roots shallow.

"They're not native," Andy said leaping onto a horizontal trunk. "They only survive here because of people watering their lawns."

I knew as much. "The palms aren't native either, but they're fine."

"True, that." He grinned. "That's because they're skinny. If we were trees, I'd be standing tall and you'd be flat on your ass."

I had no good comeback, so I resorted to giving his a leg a nudge. His arms flailed searching for his lost balance, but he didn't fall, I made sure of that.

If I weren't so focused on Andy, I would've noticed trouble approaching.

"Jon!" My name, spoken in that familiar voice, soared through the air and landed in the middle of my chest with the precision of a guided missile.

"Jon?" That was Andy looking at me and at my too-tight grip on his calf.

I let go, and he hopped off. I should've grabbed him and fled, but I didn't. We're prisoners of habits and good manners. I plastered smile on my face while Kevin and his friend strolled up to us. Kevin was the opposite of Andy, with his wide shoulders and dark hair. He hadn't changed much since I'd last seen him. He had the same blinding smile too. He presented the blond man at his side as Max, his *partner*. I pretended no to notice how his eyes flashed at me as he said the word, and shook hands with Max.

"Jon and I are old friends," Kevin explained to him.

Such a lie. We'd been more and less, but never exactly friends. I hadn't seen him or talked to him in years. And the last words we had exchanged were as far from friendly as you can get.

"And I thought I knew all of your friends." Max had a jovial smile that made his plain features more attractive. He was about the same size as Kevin but softer around the edges and older, around forty. He seemed pleasant enough. If Kevin hadn't told him about our disastrous affair, I sure wasn't going to.

"We lost touch," I said and introduced *Lea*—"rhymes with tea"—as my roommate, and they could make of that whatever they wished.

Kevin took charge of the conversation. "Jon and I used to work construction together. I jumped ship before the whole housing crash. There's more job security in building sets for TV shows."

Max put his arm around Kevin's waist. "That's how we met."

"Oh, really? What do you do?" I asked to be polite.

"I'm an editor. At various TV shows. Not very glamorous, I'm afraid. What about you?"

"Gone back to college. PCC." I inclined my head in the general direction of the campus.

"Good for you. In an economy like this, getting a degree is a smart thing to do. It'll pay off on the long run. What are you studying?"

"Advertising design."

He gave an approving nod, and made generic noises about

the advertising industry being a lucrative business. The more I listened to him, the more I got the impression he was utterly vanilla, but not a bad egg. I remembered Kevin as the adventurous type, but maybe he'd slowed down.

"Are you a student too?" Kevin smiled at Andy more affably than I remembered being his style.

"I'm a psychic," Andy said simply.

"But he doesn't tell fortunes," I added.

Kevin looked from one of us to the other. His eyes narrowed. "Then what is it you *do* do?"

"I find lost pets, mostly," Andy said.

"Sounds exciting," Kevin replied, but I saw the strain of keeping his face straight. He redirected his gaze at me. "Jon, you look good. I heard about the accident. So terrible. I'm sorry."

I didn't want to talk about it. Not with him, not then. "Thank you. You're looking good too." I meant it too.

He grimaced, but I could tell he liked the compliment. "What are you doing in Pasadena today of all days?" he asked.

"I moved here at the end of summer, to be close to school. What about you?"

"Max has a house in South Pasadena. You should see it—it's a beauty." He looped his arm around Max's as he talked. "Right now a tree is blocking the driveway, so we decided to make a long weekend of it. But first we came out to survey the wreckage. What crazy weather!"

We all agreed on that point and chatted on about the weather, real estate, the usual stuff. When we parted, Kevin insisted we had to get together sometime soon, now that we were neighbors. Andy was included in the invitation, of course. Max concurred, taking his lead from Kevin. We even exchanged phone numbers. I agreed, but had no intention of keeping my word.

***

"So you know people, after all. I was beginning to think I lived with a hermit," Andy said when we were finally alone again.

"Look who's talking, Mr. Social Butterfly."

My clunky attempt at humor didn't fool him. "Good looking guy."

"If you say so. Hey look, the clean-up crew is here."

"Why are they wearing orange?"

"Read the back of their shirts."

"*CDCR Prisoner.* Oh, you mean they're like a chain gang?"

"Well, not exactly, but sort of."

The men descended on a tree blocking two lanes of traffic. We watched them for a while, then wandered around some more till we found an open hole-in-the-wall noodle restaurant. We ordered jasmine tea to start, and Andy cradled the cup in his bare hand, but then put it down and pulled his gloves back on.

It was just too much for me to keep my trap shut. "What is up with you and those gloves?"

"Nothing. It'll pass." He took his hands off the table and hid them under it. Like it made any damn difference.

"Don't *nothing* me. You're the one insisting on being friends. So if you're acting like a squirrel fresh out of nuts, I want to know why."

He took a deep breath. "It's the Santa Anas. They enhance my sensitivity."

"What do you mean?"

"Any other time it takes an effort for me to tune into the emotions. But after the Santa Ana winds I keep picking up stray vibes from things I touch."

"Vibes? That cup is giving you vibes?"

"Yeah. It's angry."

"Angry? The cup?"

"Well, it must have picked the mood up from someone who handled it recently. The waitress or the dishwasher. I don't know."

It had to be a nuisance o feel so much just from touching... Touching, of which we'd done quite a lot of recently. "Wait a minute, this morning, when we—"

Andy cut me short. "Lust, lots of lust. And longing." A shade of pink crept up on his neck.

"You could feel what I felt?"

"Only shades of emotions. It's not like I could read your thoughts." He kept his eyes down, and the rosy tone flooded his face.

"Don't lie. Your ears are burning."

"I...uhm...saw kinkier stuff—fantasies, I suppose. Which, by the way, I'd be totally okay with."

I laughed, as much as from relief as from seeing his sheepish expression. I didn't mind him peeking into my erotic imagination. There was nothing there a couple of consenting adults would have to be bothered about.

Andy's color faded from crimson to pink. "You're not angry? It'll go away in a few days, and I'll be back to normal."

"No I'm not angry, but I don't think you'll ever be normal. But that's okay."

He winked. *"I am but mad north-north-west: when the wind is southerly I know a hawk from a handsaw."*

"What's that from? It sounds familiar."

"Haven't you read Hamlet?"

"In high school. What a twit."

"Twit?"

"Sure. He gets a whole bunch of people killed, just because he wants the throne but is too much of a candy-ass to off his uncle. That's taking passive aggression to a whole new level, don't you think?"

His eyes open wide with an incredulous glare. "I guess you really don't like Shakespeare."

"I've never much thought about it, one way or the other."

He snorted. "Yeah, clearly." He shook his head. "By the way, when are we getting a Christmas tree? We can split the cost."

"I'm not getting one."

"Why not?"

"I don't see the point. Too much hassle to put one up and load it up with decorations, just so it can dry out and shed on the floor. Then a couple of weeks later you have to drag the carcass to the curb. A waste of time and effort for what?" None of that had stopped me in the past—Alicia had delighted in the whole process and her excitement had swept me along. However, this year my holiday spirit had gone missing.

"You're a regular Grinch, aren't you?"

"And proud of it."

***

The electricity came back that evening, at least in our neighborhood. Andy and I watched TV wrapped in blankets till the apartment got back to normal temperature. According to the evening news, it would be a couple of days before the whole valley was restored to full power. The vagaries of the weather had become a field day for reporters who roamed the streets in hungry packs. The tastiest scoop they found was also the strangest. A shocked homeowner had discovered the skeletal remains of a child among the upturned roots of a large oak tree in her front yard. She notified the authorities, who promptly arrived at the scene and removed the bones. The newscaster informed us that the police were investigating the case. Considering that tree's estimated age was around a hundred, I doubted they'd uncover much.

I knew from the way Andy sat up straighter and stopped chewing his popcorn that the story tickled his fancy.

"Don't even think about it," I told him.

He swallowed and tried to look innocent. "I don't know what you mean."

"Ha. You're probably contemplating calling Lipkin and asking if he could smuggle you a finger bone. Am I right or am I right?" Detective Lipkin had been agreeably absent from our lives since October, and I preferred him to remain so.

"You're wrong! I was wondering if he could smuggle me to the morgue or wherever they keep those bones." He grinned triumphantly.

"What on earth for? Whoever put that kid in the ground is long dead."

"Wouldn't you like to know the truth?"

"The truth is overrated." Hell, I didn't want to know half the things I already did.

"You're quite the grump, aren't you?"

True, but that wasn't the point. "Your problem is that you feel too much and think too little. I remember how tense communing with those dead girls made you, and how frustrated you were afterwards. What do you expect this time? Nice people don't bury children under trees in their backyards. And whoever it was, whatever happened there's not a damn thing you can do about it after all this time. So why put yourself through that again?"

The sudden gloom of his expression made me feel like a jerk, despite knowing I was right. "C'mon, let's watch the *Cooking Channel*. Maybe we can catch Gordon Ramsey swearing up a storm." God knew, he was on all the time. If I turned on the faucet I half expected him to come out of instead of water.

"No, not him. He gives me stress."

We ended up watching a series of shows about holiday food preparations. Turkey and cranberry sauce, that kind of stuff. Andy, the hopeless food-porn addict, watched them with his eyes alight. I ignored my sense of unease the best I could. Christmas was right around the bend and nothing would stop it from hurtling through our lives with an explosion of tinsel and obligatory cheer. I just didn't know what to do about it.

Chapter Two

I didn't expect to see or hear from Kevin any time soon, if ever. So it took me unawares when he called a mere two days later on Saturday. Especially since the call wasn't for me.

Andy's face showed surprise too at first, but he became more alert as the conversation went on. "Wait, I'll ask him," he said, looking at me. "Kevin's asking if we'll drop by for coffee."

"What? Why?"

"He'd love to," Andy said into the phone.

"Hey, wait a minute," I protested, but too late. He hung up.

"Why ask me at all?" I grumbled.

"Oh c'mon, it'll be a nice walk." He was putting on his jacket and gloves already.

I couldn't forbid him to go, but there was something fishy about the whole thing, and I wanted to find out what.

When we arrived, Max and Kevin were on the sidewalk in front of their place, chatting with a neighbor, who departed just as we arrived.

Max must've done well for himself, because the house had to be worth a big bundle of money in that part of town, even in this market. And even with half of a tree blocking the driveway.

"Nice house," I told Max. "Lucky that the tree missed the roof."

"No kidding. I had the car parked out there, but moved it into the garage when the wind picked up. It would've been flattened. Of course, now I can't drive anywhere." His smile suggested no distress over the fact.

"Doesn't Kevin know how to operate a chainsaw?" I asked. He was a carpenter after all.

Kevin punched me in the shoulder. "Shhh! If that was

public knowledge, not only would our long weekend have been shot, but I'd be spending a short one chopping trees. I've never liked chainsaws, anyway. They're all made for right-handed people, which I'm not. So shall we go?"

"Go where?" I asked befuddled.

"Didn't Lea tell you? That tree from the news, you know with the child skeleton, is down the next street. We'll go have a look-see."

"No. He forgot to mention it." I turned to Andy with a dirty look, but the scheming scamp was already walking down the street in animated conversation with Max.

Kevin and I took off after them, but Kevin kept stopping, checking out the damage to other people's yards, till we lagged several paces behind.

"So how did you two meet?" he asked out of the blue.

"Through an ad."

"Really? I would've never guessed you to go for the personals. What did it say? Single white gay man looking for psychic twink? Must have bubble butt?"

"Roommate wanted," I said while keeping my eye on Andy. He did have a bubble butt.

"Oh, don't tell me you're not doing it like rabbits."

I said nothing.

Kevin smirked with triumph. "That's what I thought. So not your type, but then again maybe he's exactly that. You were always a sucker for a damsel in distress, just not in men. When did you switch?"

"When did you turn into a bitch queen?" I cut back.

He shot me a sharp glare. "Oh, I dunno, I guess when I realized you'd never leave your wife for me. Such an old fashioned melodrama, weren't we?"

"You always knew I wouldn't leave Alicia."

What had happened between me and Kevin had been entirely my fault. I broke all my rules getting involved with someone from our circle of friends, and most of all getting involved emotionally. I should've stopped it when it had become clear we'd been having more than just great sex. I hadn't and it'd blown up in our faces.

Clearly, Kevin still bore the scars. "Yeah, you told me. I didn't believe you. We had something, didn't we?"

It was no good picking at those scabs now. "Alicia needed me more." Kevin never understood, and never would.

"Of course, Saint Alicia—"

"Don't," I snapped, and he clamped his lips together.

He didn't say a word till we'd almost reached our destination. "Sorry. Let's have a truce, okay?"

"Fine by me. Max seems like a nice guy," I said, by way of offering an olive branch.

"He is."

The gathering of people around on the sidewalk was too small and well-mannered to be called a crowd. They acted with the obligatory nonchalance of the middle-aged and wealthy, but their intermittent glances toward a fallen tree shone with the excitement of children. Andy, on the other hand, had none of their composure. He stared like a kid in a candy store.

I stepped up to him. "It's just a tree. The police must have taken anything relevant."

"I know that," he said, looking at me. "I'd like to take a look anyway."

"Fine, knock yourself out."

The owner of the house and tree turned out to be an older woman. She and Andy chatted for a few minutes, then he cut across the lawn. I noticed he'd taken off his gloves, and wondered what the devil he was up to. Even the dignified folks around us started to stare when Andy leaned across the tree, pressing his face and hands to the bark.

"Your boyfriend is quite a tree hugger," Kevin snickered.

I could've enlightened him about the nature of our relationship, but he was pissing me off enough that I didn't.

When Andy didn't move for minutes, the people stared conversing with each other again, pointedly not making remarks on the spectacle. Yet the moment Andy stood and ambled back, they all went quiet.

Andy hunched his shoulders like when he was tired, but his expression showed no tension.

"All right. Spit it out," Kevin demanded.

"Oh." Andy pinked under all the gazes directed at him. "It wasn't a kid, but a small person."

Several pairs of eyebrows rose in unison, including mine.

And Kevin's. "You mean a dwarf?"

"Uhm, well, yes, but you don't call them that anymore."

"Yes, yes. Who killed him?"

Andy bit his lip. "A horse. A big white horse. Sorry, that's all I have."

A girl of ten or so stared at Andy with keen interest, but her father and the rest of the adults hid their reactions ranging from doubt to disdain behind polite smiles. It was time for us to exit stage left. With a hand around his arm I tugged Andy out of the circle of their attention.

My plan was to go straight home, but Andy turned to Max with a smile. "I was promised a coffee."

Max nodded. "Yes of course, we should go, shouldn't we?"

***

Kevin maneuvered himself to walk next to Andy, so I got stuck with Max. We talked about the weather, gas prices, and the Anaheim Ducks—Max was into hockey. I only half paid attention to him, as I was listening in on the conversation going on between Kevin and Andy.

Kevin started the chat. "That was quite an impressive performance out there. You know, you could make much better money channeling people's dead relatives than looking for their lost pets." An edge hid under the velvet of his voice, and I didn't like it.

"I'm not a medium," Andy protested.

"You did pretty well."

"All I got was a few faint impressions."

"From a tree. That's quite feat, wouldn't you say? You could go on TV with tricks like that."

"I don't normally—" Andy started but I pushed myself between them.

"That's enough psychic chatter for today," I said and pulled Andy forward. "Do you want to just go home?" I asked him in a whisper. He shook his head.

I didn't want to be rude to Max and I thought Andy could use a chance to rest. He leaned heavily on me as we walked back to the house. Pasadena in general has some of the best looking residential architecture in the city, and South Pasadena in particular has a high concentration of it. This was an affluent neighborhood with an old world charm. The neighborhood council would probably have anyone shot if they tried building a McMansion there. Max's modest, two-story Craftsman-style home nestled among shrubs and tall trees. With its green, wood shingle siding and brown eaves the house fit perfectly. The interior matched in style—no ugly modernization.

"Nice place," I remarked, as we settled in the living room.

"Isn't it?" Kevin said beaming with pride, as if he built it himself. He put the tray of coffee on the table before doling out the individual cups. "Max inherited it from his father, who got it from his father." He put a mug in front of Andy, who was still pulling his gloves off.

I watched Andy cautiously pick it up, but seeing no signs of discomfort, I turned my attention to Max. "Really? It must've been nice growing up in such a stylish home."

He chuckled. "As a kid I saw it as a drag. My father would cuff me on the ears if I as much as scraped the wood," he said, motioning at the wooden beams and built-in cabinets.

We had small talk about the challenges in historical home maintenance, and fighting off termites. At least after a decade in construction it was a subject familiar to me. Max and Kevin were easy around each other. I didn't miss how as he talked Max kept touching Kevin on the arm and shoulder. When he looked at Kevin affection shone from his eyes.

Thankfully, Kevin stopped needling Andy. When the conversation turned to Max's grandfather, who had the house built, he added, "He was quite the character, at least from what I heard." He prodded Max. "Hun, you should show them the picture. You know the one with all of you."

Max obediently got up and retrieved a frame photograph from the other room. He held it out to Andy who sat closest. Andy took the photo from him but dropped it right away. It landed on the coffee table with a big *thunk*.

"I'm so sorry!" Andy squeaked, tucking his hands around himself.

I picked the picture up by its heavy silver frame. No wonder it made such a noise. "Everything's fine, the glass didn't break," I said to calm him. Max and Kevin were unruffled.

I held the black and white photo so Andy could see it. In the picture a white-haired old man stood in the middle of the group. A large, well-kept mustache and a roguish smile decorated his wizened face. To his left stood a young woman in a dress that screamed seventies, complete with floppy hat and huge sunglasses. On the other side of the old guy stood a severe-faced man. The only allowance he'd given to the fashion of the time was the wide lapels of his suit. A boy of four or five standing up front completed the family assembly. His grin mirrored the old man's.

"Your parents?" I asked Max.

"Yes. The best picture I have of them. We had a ton of color photos but they've all turned purple."

"Black and white photographs are more archival. Especially compared to the early commercial color processes." I'd learned that in my art history class. We'd touched on photography toward the end of the semester.

"It's also the only photo I have with the five of us. Grandpa died few months after the picture was taken. I don't remember much of him, except from the stories my mother told."

"Max was such a cute kid, wasn't he?" Kevin asked.

Studying the grinning boy in the photo, I had to agree. Andy nodded too as he leaned against me. I gave him a sideway glance—he looked more worn out than he did at the tree. I suggested we head out, and he didn't object.

***

Andy didn't say much during the walk, and as soon as we got home, he threw himself on the sofa.

"You look like crap. Put your feet up. Want some tea?" I asked.

"Chamomile with honey, please."

Nothing in the friends-with-benefits arrangement said I couldn't make him tea. He'd even done it for me before. When I returned from the kitchen, Andy still lay on the couch, but with a blanket wrapped around him. I plonked myself in a chair and watched him sip his drink.

"I had no idea you could get a psychic reading cuddling a tree. You're full of surprises," I said.

"I normally wouldn't. It's the wind, making me extra sensitive."

"Still?"

"It's going away, I can feel it." He massaged his temple with one hand. "And the headache coming to take its place."

"Want an aspirin?"

"Wouldn't help. I'll just have to ride it out."

"Is it always like this?" There was so much I didn't know,

only that what he did took a toll on him.

He cupped his hands around the warm mug. "It's part of the big equation. You don't get psychic superpowers without paying for them. Although, I'd rather not have them at all. It's too much, and I keep getting ambushed. Like with Max."

That was news to me. "Max? What happened?"

"When he handed me the photo our fingers touched, and I got a flash."

"A flash of what?"

Andy sipped more tea. "Hard to describe. Sorrow? Remorse? Definitely something unhappy. It came as a shock, that's why I dropped the picture. Max seems such a nice guy, and the coffee cup felt content—like a lazy Sunday afternoon." He slid the empty mug onto the coffee table and burrowed deeper under the blanket.

"A lot of people have regrets in their pasts."

"I know that. His felt so sharp." He pressed the heels of his hands to his eyes. "Hell, it was probably simply my sensitivity spiking. Stupid wind."

"I'm sorry about Kevin being a dick," I said.

He squinted at me. "You were lovers, weren't you?"

"Years ago. It ended badly, but I thought he'd be over it by now."

"He still has feelings for you, but he's pissed too. That must've been some breakup."

"You touched him too?"

"Please. A piece of rock could've picked that up. When we walked to the tree, and you two lagged behind, talking—well, when you caught up your face was like thunder."

"I didn't think you noticed anything but the tree."

"Well, I did. It wasn't my business, and still isn't…"

"But?"

"It doesn't add up. You, Kevin, your wife."

It wouldn't to most people, unless you knew the whole story. "Alicia and I tied the knot when we were eighteen. It meant we could cut lose from our families start our own lives, and we needed each other for support."

"You could've done that without getting married."

"Legally, that piece of paper made all the difference. Alicia had a fear she might end up in a hospital and her mother would be the one making life and death decisions for her."

"That bad?"

"She was a manipulative bitch, and a compulsive liar."

"But how did you…"

"What?"

"You know, sex?"

"That we didn't do. I've never been attracted to women, and Alicia had no interest in physical intimacy at all." It still filled me with sadness and frustration that such basic pleasure had been taken away from her. "She'd been molested by her stepfather since she was little. The slimy asshole did it so insidiously, she had no idea what was coming till it was too late, and by then she couldn't tell anyone because of the guilt. The fucking asshole really messed her up."

"Son of a bitch! I'd want to kill him."

"I would've, but by the time she was able to tell me, cancer had already taken care of him. Small justice. The end of it was that Alicia didn't want to have sex at all, even after all the therapy."

"And you?"

"I had affairs on the side. Nothing serious. She knew. We even had a code name for it—poker night with the boys. You think it's fucked up, don't you?"

"A little, but it's not my place to judge."

"Damn right."

"And Kevin?"

"I made a mistake letting things go too far. It got serious."

"Did you ever consider divorce?"

"Not then. But later Alicia and I talked about it." Mostly she did. "I wasn't comfortable with the idea till she was well enough, physically and emotionally." She'd seemed getting to be there just before that fucking visit and the accident.

I rubbed my face—I'd started feeling tired too, or at least emotionally drained.

***

On Sunday morning Andy didn't come out of his room, even for breakfast. He said he wasn't hungry. So I let him be. I had a whole lot of studying and paper writing to do since finals were right around the corner. When my brain couldn't take it anymore, I went to campus. Not many people go there on Sundays, so I could have the drawing studio to myself. We all had the option to enter a piece in the end of semester student art show. I wanted to create something original for it, but wasn't sure what.

On a whim I decided to recreate from memory the Polaroid photo Lipkin showed us—the one with the two girls and the bundle. I cut a long strip from the thirty-six-inch wide roll of Strathmore paper I had, and tacked it up on the wall. After working on the charcoal drawing for over an hour, I stepped back and realized bigger wasn't always better. However, I liked the wide format—it reminded me of wide screen movies. I cut a twenty-two-inch strip of paper, put it on the wall horizontally, and began to work.

The finished piece had an undeniably eerie mood. The blurry features of the girls from the photograph gained an ominous quality in my rendition. They stood to one side, while at the other edge of the frame was a man whose face you couldn't see, only the back of his head and his shoulder. In the background stretched a narrow road. After lengthy deliberation I decided it was as good as it was ever going to be. I sprayed the drawing with fixative and carefully rolled it up. I figured I'd enter it in the student show.

I drove home under a bruised sky as the sun slipped below the horizon. Opening the door to the apartment, it struck me how empty and lifeless it felt without the signs of another person there. No murmur of television, no clatter in the kitchen, and especially no slender figure stretched out on the couch, face buried in a book. The pang of desolation stabbed me between the ribs.

Dropping my bag, I went to investigate. I had no reason to worry, yet my heart jumped into my throat. Andy's door was open a crack and I pushed it wider. The curtains were drawn and the lights were off. I could hardly make out the still shape on the bed.

"Are you all right?" I whispered into the darkness.

The figure stirred and a muzzy voice replied, "I'm fine. Just feeling lazy today."

I hadn't realized how tense my muscles had been till that moment of relief. "Have you eaten?"

"Not hungry." He pulled a pillow over his head.

I left him, grumbling about ungrateful brats, but returned half an hour later with a bowl of soup.

Andy snapped at me as I turned the bedside lamp on. "Stop fussing, Jon. I can make my own soup."

"You wouldn't know how to open the can. Which is a crying shame after watching all those foodie shows. You're worse than a monk addicted to Internet porn. Now shut up, sit up, and eat."

He grumbled, but pushed himself up and took the bowl. How he managed to get dark circles around his eyes from lying in bed all day I had no idea.

"You look like something the cat threw up," I said.

He shrugged, nearly spilling the hot broth. "I'm fine. Doesn't that saying go *what the cat dragged in*?"

"Possibly. How's the head?"

"Fine."

"Really?" I packed my voice full of accusation.

He gave me an innocent look from under his lashes. I wasn't buying it and glared back. He sighed. "Fine. I had a splitting migraine, but it's gone now. I'm just tired."

I shook my head. "You could've told me."

"I didn't want you to fuss. I hate people fussing over me."

"I don't fuss."

He shook as if trying not to laugh. "Sure, Jon," he said and returned his attention to the soup.

While he ate, I looked around the room. He'd finally unpacked the rest of his books, but now they sat in big piles against the wall.

"I was wondering," Andy said between slurps.

"About what?"

"About how the little guy ended up under a tree. Such a strange thing."

***

We never found out the exact answer to that question, but a week later the Sunday paper divulged new information. I wasn't surprised in the slightest to learn Andy had been right—the bones belonged not to an child, but an adult male suffering from dwarfism. Someone must've lit a fire under the coroner's ass to get the results so fast.

"It says the cause of death was blunt force trauma to the head," I said, lowering the paper.

Andy looked up from his paperback. "Does the article say what did it?"

"No."

"I'm starting to think he worked in a circus."

"Are you making this up, or know something?"

He laid the book on his chest. "When I close my eyes and think of him, I see a white horse with feathers on its head, but I have no idea if it's a psychic impression or my own imagination. Maybe if I had a chance to see the bones… I could ask Detective Lipkin." A speculative glint appeared in his eyes.

I rushed to put it out. "Leave Lipkin alone. The police don't need your help in an ancient case. And I don't want you to see him behind my back either."

Andy laughed. "You make it sound like he and I are having a torrid affair."

The bizarreness of the image made me grin. Lipkin was straighter than a gun barrel. My gaze strayed to the framed drawing above the couch. It hadn't been my idea to hang it there, or even frame it. "Doesn't it bother you?" I asked, staring at the two girls with the bundle.

"No. It's nice."

"Nice?"

"Yeah. The way you draw them…I dunno…Mysterious. Sometimes I stare at them and think of their story as a book."

Chapter Three

Kevin called. He wanted to meet, just him and me, and I reluctantly agreed. Starbucks served as neutral ground. He was already there when I arrived, squeezed behind a tiny table. I got me a plain coffee, and braced myself.

However, he didn't hurry—his gaze lingered on me over the rim of his cup, as if taking stock. "You've changed," he said, putting the cup down. "You've always been serious, but now…"

"What?"

"Like you forgot how to have fun."

"The past year hasn't been a bed of roses." I caught myself drumming on the table with my fingers, and tried to put a lid on my annoyance.

Kevin leaned forward and the tenderness in his eyes reminded me of why I loved him once. "I know. I'm sorry. After I heard about the accident I wanted to visit you in the hospital, but it didn't feel right. I was still angry. I should've at least called though."

His hand lay merely an inch from mine. I picked up my coffee. "And now?"

He leaned back in his chair. "I'm trying not to be. The problem is we never had a proper closure, talked things out."

"I remember a pretty big talk."

"No, that was me shouting and you shutting down. We didn't talk things out like a couple of adults." His words carried regret and a touch of reproach.

"We were young," I reminded him.

"Look at you, old man. It was only five years ago," he said smiling.

"Six. But I feel much older."

Kevin nodded and played with his cup. "Has it ever

occurred to you that maybe it wasn't an accident?"

"What do you mean?"

"She tried to kill herself before."

"That was an accidental overdose."

"Oh, Jon…" He shook his head and stared out the window for a moment. "Forget I said anything. I don't want to fight. None of it matters now, anyway. After we split I had a string of bad relationships and realized how hard it is for two people to make a go of it. I came to almost admire what you and Alicia had."

"Almost?"

"Give me a break. I have a right to be jealous. Especially now. First time I see you in years, and you're with a hot twink."

"And you're with Max."

"Max and I are like a couple of fuzzy slippers—lots of comfort, but short on passion."

"Don't knock comfort."

"Purely hypothetically, do you think if we were both free agents we could have another shot?"

I had wondered about that myself before—there was a reason I hadn't tried to catch up with him once in five years. "We have too much water under the bridge."

He snorted. "That's not how the saying goes."

"You're probably right."

"You've always butchered them—it used to drive me crazy. I have a confession to make. Us meeting the other day wasn't completely by accident."

"What do you mean?"

"I knew where you lived. I looked you up after hearing through the grapevine you moved to Pasadena. It's a small town, we were bound to run into each other sooner or later, but after the winds I suggested to Max we walk in that direction."

"Why?"

"I dunno. Curiosity? Obsession? Whatever it was, I'm over it, I promise. There's no undoing the past, right? Lea…I didn't see it at first, but he makes sense for you. He needs looking after, and it's your thing."

"Don't start."

"I'm not trying to be an ass, I swear. You were born to be a big brother, to take care of someone. You try to pretend you're not, but it's in your blood."

"Bullshit."

He shook his head. "You're such an idiot sometimes. Anyway, I want to make up to Leander for being snippy with him. At first I thought he was a baby-faced grifter, bamboozling foolish old you. But apparently, he's the real deal. Who woulda thought? My jaw fell to the floor when I read in the paper about the dwarf. Is he always like that?"

"He has his moments."

"You don't say. The two of you should come over this Saturday. We'll have our annual pre-holiday de-stressing party. A bunch of the neighbors will be there. These are posh people who lose shit all the time, and are too damn pampered to look for anything themselves. Lea could pick up some good business there."

"I'll ask him."

***

We showed up at Max's house Saturday afternoon. The party hadn't started swinging yet, but it was gathering momentum. I recognized a few faces from the time we'd looked at the skeleton tree. They recognized us too, especially Andy. I noted inquisitive looks and whispered exchanges.

True to his word, Kevin greeted us with open arms. "I'm glad you could make it. Food's in the dining room, drinks in the kitchen." He latched onto Andy. "Jon, why don't you put your coats in the guest bedroom? It's that way. I want to introduce Leander to some friends."

He towed Andy away, and I did as told. Wandering around, I noted the lack of holiday decorations, aside from the fairy lights hanging everywhere. Clearly, I wasn't the only one not into the whole fuss. The dining room table offered a bounty of hot dogs and sausages, piled on a row of plates. According to the handwritten cards identifying them, they ranged from tofu to duck. I picked an old-fashioned bratwurst and decorated it with spicy pepper and mustard, ignoring the more exotic options like the Thai peanut sauce. After procuring a mug of hot apple cider too, I returned to the living room where I was lucky enough to snag an armchair in the corner. It was a comfortable old thing, the seat cushion displaying a permanent groove.

From my roost I had a good view of the whole room and Andy mingling with the other guests. He moved among them awkwardly at first, but gradually, and with Kevin's help, he relaxed. Soon he stood, glass of wine in one hand, in the middle of a circle of admirers. As one of them leaned forward asking a question, Andy handed him a business card. Others took them too. I hadn't even known Andy had business cards. Came to show you how little I knew.

"He's twisting them around his little finger, isn't he?" Max brought a wooden folding chair with him, which he set up next to mine.

"Leander's good at that. Nice party."

"Thanks. Everyone's so stressed out around this time of year, it's good to have a chance to blow off steam. We keep it simple, no potluck to bring and no gifts to exchange."

"I see. That explains the menu."

"Exactly. Throwing hot dogs on the grill is as simple as it gets, but having a variety of them makes it fancier than plain old burgers."

"Smart."

"Usually we do a bigger production, but we didn't have the energy this time around with all the packing. We're off to Barbados for the holidays."

"Wow, nice!"

"So much to do before, though. We'll leave on Wednesday, and I'll have to go to the airport straight from work."

"Well, give yourself enough time. The security will be hell, I bet."

His face sagged. "I know. Oh, the joys of being treated like cattle."

I felt bad for wrecking his good mood. "Cheer up and enjoy the moment." I lifted my mug and clinked it against his wine glass.

While we talked more guests arrived, and Kevin went to greet them, leaving Andy on his own. Andy was doing fine, though, chatting with ease. He clearly didn't need Kevin's help anymore. Or mine. I saw him getting into an animated discussion with a man I remembered from two weeks ago— he was the one whose daughter had watched Andy with such keen interest.

"Are all the other guests neighbors?" I asked Max.

"Yes. That way if they drink too much, they can stagger home on foot, no driving involved. Oh, did you drive?"

I nodded. It was only twenty minute on foot, but I'd opted for wheels. "We could've hoofed it, but I'd rather not walk home in the dark."

"Yes, of course. Sorry for not inviting you when you came by last time, but I didn't even think of it."

"Don't worry about it."

"After reading the article about the skeleton, Kevin felt mortified. We both had our doubts about Leander before, I hope you understand."

"So did I."

"He's the real deal, isn't he? Hard to believe. I mean,

getting that from a tree." He shook his head. "It boggles the mind."

"He isn't always like that. The Santa Ana winds enhanced his abilities. He was picking up impressions just from touching things. It's gone now."

Max blinked at me. "Really? He can do that?"

"Well, not anymore, thank God."

Max smiled politely, but his mind seemed elsewhere. He pushed himself up. "Excuse me, I need to check on the food."

He dashed off, and I decided to be more sociable myself. I made my way to Andy's side just as a woman handed him a lone earring. It had lots of sparkly stones, and I bet none of them were cubic zirconia.

"I have no idea where the other one is. I even thought maybe the maid stole it, but that's ridiculous—why would anyone steal only one earring? And Rosa wouldn't do that anyway. Could you please give it a try? I know I'm being rude asking you here, but it was my mother's."

Looking her over I saw she was no spring chicken, but she'd held up nice, with curves in all the right places and red hair framing an oval face.

"No problem, Anjelica." Cupping his hands around the earring, Andy bowed his head. His eyelids slipped closed.

The group around us hushed, and the quiet spread around the room, and I only heard a murmur of voices.

A minute or so later Andy looked up and at Anjelica. "We should go to your house. It's not far, right?"

"Right across the street."

He redirected his blue gaze at me. "Jon, would you help me?"

I slipped my hand under his arm, and he leaned on me while we walked out of the house, across the road, and into another house. Anjelica and her husband marched in front of us. Andy's steps faltered as he closed his eyes again, but I made sure he didn't fall on his face. After a hesitant moment in the foyer we led each other into the kitchen. Sensing that we'd reached our destination, I let go of his arm.

After standing still for what seemed like forever, but probably only a couple of minutes, he crouched in front of the fridge. "There you are!"

The husband and I moved the big stainless steel thing with some effort. It weighed a ton. Underneath we found the piece of jewelry in question.

"How the hell did it get there?" asked the husband, whose name I still didn't know.

Andy spread his hands. "I can find them but have no idea how they ended up where they did."

"I feel such a fool now. And to think I almost accused Rosa," Anjelica said blushing. "Oh, we should pay you. Fred, get your checkbook."

Andy stopped him. "That won't be necessary. It's almost Christmas, after all. Call me if you lose anything else." He handed her a business card with a smile. *Smooth.*

"Oh, I sure will. I'll tell all my friends too."

***

She started singing Andy's praises as soon as we got back to the party. Feeling superfluous, I retreated to the sidelines. I partook in a conversation about football and gas prices, till an old codger got hold of me. Archie, as he introduced himself, launched into the history of the neighborhood. He'd lived there all his life, as I soon learned. I asked him about the skeleton tree.

He wrinkled his already heavily lined face. "It was an empty lot when I was a kid, but I'm fairly sure the tree was already there. The Wadsworths built the house, but they moved to Orange County in the seventies. Those were some rough times then. Lots of crime. Many of the old neighbors moved away." I nodded politely, and he took it as an encouragement to ramble on. "Max's folk stayed—old Tom Finnegan loved this house too much. He wouldn't give it up. His father, Max's grandfather built it, you know."

"Yes, I knew that."

"For a few years there were three generations of the Finnegans living under one roof. Nowadays people don't do that. I have three daughters and they flew off in three different directions. One lives in New York. Can you imagine that? All that dirt, and traffic, and the people are so rude. I couldn't live there. My other daughter, Angie, she lives here in L.A., in an apartment. I told her she should move in with me, the house is big enough, but no, she *needs her space*. That's young people these days, scattering in all directions of the wind.

I scrambled to fit in a few words edgewise before he could hurtle into another rant. "I saw a photo of Max with his parents and grandfather. They were an interesting family."

He flipped his wrist. "Nah, you got it wrong. That couldn't have been Max. He wasn't born till after old Vernon Finnegan died."

"But I saw him in the picture."

"That must've been Max's brother."

"I didn't know he had a brother." Of course, I barely knew anything about him.

Archie was eager to fill me in. "Oh yes, Felix. Now there was a rascal if God ever made one. He took after his grandpa, I'm afraid. Old Vernon was a regular rabble-rouser back in the day. Felix was the same, always up to no good. I remember when he dyed Mrs. Madison's cat blue. He got a good hiding for it too—Tom was a strict man. Didn't stop Felix none. But he got away with a lot of mischief, especially with the women folk. He was a charmer, like I haven't seen since. He left a lot of broken-hearted girls behind when he ran off with their maid. What was her name? Mary…no, Maria."

That got my flagging attention. "He ran off?"

"He sure did. He was only eighteen then, and she was older, in her twenties, but nobody was surprised. Felix had that effect on women of all ages."

He went on in that vein, regaling me with the exploits of young Felix, which led to stories about other neighbors. The old man knew some juicy gossip, even if most of it was decades old. He seemed happy to have an audience, and all I needed to do was nod occasionally to keep him going. I zoned out at some point, but I didn't think he noticed.

As the night wore on, the party began to thin out. People started to leave in ones and twos. My old buddy Archie had dozed off. I cast my gaze around for Andy but couldn't see him. I wandered through the kitchen and checked the bathroom, without luck. Finally, I found him in the back of the house, in the laundry room. He stood with his head bowed, lost in a trance in front of a wooden door, his hand on the brass doorknob. If I'd had a doubt of him doing one of his psychic things, his bare feet would've been a dead giveaway.

"Leander!"

He jumped at the sound of my voice, but tried to recover. "Hey."

"What are you doing?"

"Nothing. Admiring the architectural details." His face colored even as he said the words.

"Yeah, right. Snooping around in your host's house is plain rude. Didn't they teach you that in psychic school?"

"I wasn't—"

"Put your shoes on. It's time to go," I said and went to collect our coats.

***

We said our goodbyes and agreed to meet again sometime next year.

My prickly mood followed me into the car. "You're such a terrible liar," I grumbled.

"All right, I'm sorry about snooping. Sheesh."

"What about that woman's earring?"

"What about it?"

"Don't tell me you didn't know how it ended up under the fridge."

"Oh."

"I knew it!"

"That's different. She wouldn't have liked her husband to find out. And I won't tell you anything else either. There's such thing as psychic-client confidentiality."

"There's no such thing."

"There is! An unwritten one."

"Oh, fine. I don't want to know." I really didn't. To shift the subject, I said, "Max and Kevin didn't have Christmas decorations either."

"Of course not, they'll be out of town."

"Ah, so Kevin told you."

Andy's eyes gained a dreamy sheen. "Barbados—must be nice. Max must make good money. Unless he inherited it along with the house. Ether way, it's nice to be able to travel."

"Sure is. Oh, I heard something interesting."

When I told Andy what I'd learned from Archie, he Wrinkled his face. "That's so weird. Why would Max lie about that stuff?"

"I have no idea why people do most of the things they do. Maybe it's Max in the photo and Archie got it wrong. He was pretty decrepit."

"Yeah, but Max didn't say a word about a brother. Wouldn't he at least mention he had one? I should call Kevin and ask him if he knows anything about Felix."

I immediately regretted saying anything at all about

Archie's tales. "You should do no such thing! They have enough stress getting ready for their trip without you digging up old family strife. Maybe Max and Felix had a falling out. Shit happens. God knows, I haven't talked to my own parents in years. You should let sleeping dogs the hell alone."

"Lie."

"What?"

"Let sleeping dogs lie."

"Same thing. Now promise me you won't call Kevin. Or Max."

"Fine. I won't call them. Happy?"

"Delirious."

Chapter Four

I thought I'd lost my holiday spirit for good, but it'd merely been hiding among the dust bunnies of my subconscious, only to tackle me in the shower when I was most defenseless. I reached for Andy's shampoo by accident and the concentrated scent of citrus brought back childhood memories of Christmas with my grandmother. Every year she'd made an orange chocolate cake that was to die for. I began salivating just thinking about it. And it came to me—there was no reason why I couldn't do something special for Christmas. I didn't have much to do till school started up again in January. A traditional dinner with turkey and trimmings would be nice. Maybe not a whole turkey, only the breast. I'd have Andy help. I didn't have Grandma's recipe, but I could find another one on the Internet.

Andy had gone out on a job, so I'd have to tell him about the changed plans later. I rushed off to the store more energized than I'd felt in a long time. Nothing could get me down, not the stressed-out fellow shoppers jamming their grocery carts into my kidneys, nor the cheesy holiday music polluting the air. The checkout lane was a lot like the freeway at rush hour—barely moving. I zoned out while mentally composing my to-do list. Right then an idea popped into my head—the perfect gift for Andy. So simple I should've thought of it sooner.

Back at the apartment, I put the groceries away and grabbed my tools from the storage locker downstairs. After taking the necessary measurements, I rushed off to the hardware store. By the time I'd hauled everything home, I was tuckered, and decided to take a quick nap.

I woke with a jolt and the memory of falling, and still feeling the dreadful weight of the dream. There was something wrong with Andy, I just knew it. I checked his room but I knew he wouldn't be there. He didn't answer his phone either. Any other time it wouldn't have been a big deal, but right then I had the irrational urge to find Andy. Fast. Lacking a better idea I called Kevin.

"Have you seen Andy?" I barked into the phone without saying hello.

"Not since Saturday. Why? Anything wrong?"

"I don't know. Call me if you hear from him."

"That's unlikely. I'm on my way to the airport. Max had to rush home. He forgot the passports. Can you believe it? I want to kill him."

A chill came over me as everything clicked into place—Max, the house, and Andy, curious as a cat. I hung up on Kevin and called Lipkin while running down the stairs, too much in a hurry to wait for the elevator. I left a brief message when he didn't answer, and jumped into the car.

Navigating the busy streets, I held the steering wheel so hard I thought it might crack. It took all my willpower not to slam my foot on the gas pedal and speed through a red light. The moment the lights changed I took off, way ahead of everyone. They probably thought of me as an asshole. I didn't give a flying fuck. The only thing on my mind was reaching Andy in time. An evil little shit from the darkest depths of my soul kept whispering it was too late. That I'd fucked up again, something terrible had happened. Again. And it was my fault, because I'd relaxed, let myself be happy. Fate would smack me down for such arrogance, and Andy would be the casualty.

I should've known. The most dangerous thing in the world is caring for another person. My heart was so scarred it couldn't take another blow. If anything happened to Andy, I'd find that bridge, I knew that for a fact.

***

I pulled up in front of the house in a squeal of tires. Max answered my franingbanging on the door almost immediately.

"Where's Andy?" I yelled at him.

He stared at me with face scrunched in shock and

confusion. "What are you talking about?"

I faltered, but a flash of red caught my eye through the crack of the door. I barged forward but he blocked my way. "Are you crazy? What the hell are you doing? I need to get to the airport or we'll miss the plane."

I stepped back and swung my hand. As my fist connected with his jaw, piercing pain shot up my arm. Max went down with a thud. I stepped over him, walking past Andy's red sneakers as I went. After a second of hesitation I headed for the laundry room. The door was locked so I sprinted back to Max to take his keys. He lay motionless on the floor, and I really didn't care if he was alive or dead. I grabbed the keys and rushed back to the locked door. My hands shook so hard I could barely hit the keyhole, but fortunately the fourth key opened the lock.

Blindly feeling around, I found the light switch. The single lightbulb lit a basement littered with broken furniture, old boxes, and assorted household castoffs. I sprinted down the stairs.

"Andy? Are you here?" I said as loud as I could without shouting. The panic inside me wanted to scream.

Holding my breath, I pricked my ears for any sound. Nothing at first, then a faint shuffle that could've been a mouse. I made my way in its direction, shoving aside piles of crap. Under an overturned sofa I spotted an old carpet with a human-shaped lump inside it. I scrambled to unwrap it. Andy's face was red and he took a deep breath when I removed his gag.

"Jon! How did you know?" He gasped.

I was too fucking mad to answer, so I focused on untying his legs and feet, and loosening the miles of rope wrapped around him.

"Jon?" he asked again, his gaze searching my face.

I lost it. Grabbing his shoulders, I shook him. "You pig-headed, inconsiderate son of a bitch!"

"It's nice to see you too, Jon." The warmth of his voice and smile only made me feel worse.

"I can't fucking do this." There were no words to express how fucking vulnerable I felt. I couldn't move for fear I'd shatter like glass.

Andy reached out and pulled me to him, and I managed somehow to remain in one piece. An animal sound escaped my throat as I grabbed onto him and buried my face in his shoulder.

His skinny arms held me firm. "Shhh...I'm here. I'll always be here."

"Bullshit," I sobbed. Tears ran down my face and soaked into his shirt. I was powerless to stop them.

"I'm psychic, remember?"

"And a liar."

"Shush, you."

We clung to each other till the residues of terror and anxiety drained out of me, leaving exhaustion behind.

I wiped my face with my hands. "What the hell were you thinking?"

"I was only going to walk around the house, but I saw the door open. I yelled in but there was no answer, so I thought I'd get a quick feel before calling Kevin. Next thing I knew I was flat on the ground and Max was tying me up." He gave me that look of blue-eyed innocence I was so not buying.

"Were you out of your fucking mind? You could've been killed. If you ever do anything like this again, I'll wring your neck."

The way he drew his brows together, I knew he was about to have one of his pig-headed moments. Sure thing. "Max is not a killer," he said.

"You're so wrong about that," the voice came from behind us.

I did a one-eighty and jumped to my feet, ready to fight,

but it was not necessary. Max crumpled onto the bottom step of the stairs and sat there with his head between his hands. Not feeling particularly charitable toward him, I fought the urge to give him a thrashing.

Not Andy though—the twit came forward and kneeled in front of Max to touch his arm. "Hey."

I looked on, gritting my teeth, but let Andy take the lead. As long as I was there to keep him safe.

Max shuddered. "I can't carry this anymore. I killed Maria. You should call the cops."

"I already have," I bluffed. Technically, Lipkin was a cop, but I had no idea if he'd gotten my message and how he'd taken it.

Andy pressed his palm on the concrete floor. "She's here, isn't she? Right under us."

Max nodded. "She's been in the ground since father and I put her there. Twenty-seven years."

"What happened? How did she die?"

"I didn't mean to…" Max looked up with misery-filled eyes.

"Max, start from the beginning," Andy said in soft voice.

Max didn't reply right away. His eyes glazed over and anguish twisted his expression. "I got home early from school. Mother was out. I thought the house was empty, but I heard shouting from upstairs—Maria and my father. Something about money. I remember thinking how strange it was that Maria was yelling at him like that. She was only the maid, after all. Then it got quiet. I crept upstairs." He halted and took a deep breath before going on. "The door to the bedroom was open, I could see it all. She was on her knees, with my father's dick in her mouth. The way they were, he couldn't see me, but Maria could. She winked at me and went on. I swear she was performing for me. I should've left but I was rooted to the spot. When they were done, she stood and said *Don't forget what we agreed*. And just walked out and shut the door.

Andy furrowed his brows. "What did she mean by it?"

"I've never found out. But she seemed triumphant but also sort of...I don't know...strange. She pushed me against the banister and whispered that I was a little perv, but like she was coming onto me. She grabbed my crotch too. When she found out I was soft, she got angry. She asked what was wrong with me. I just wanted to get away but she kissed me, forced her tongue in my mouth. I could taste my father's spunk on her. I was so disgusted, I shoved her away with all my strength. I didn't mean to push her down the stairs, but she fell all the way to the bottom, and then just lay there."

"Max, it was an accident, and you were, what, fourteen?"

"Thirteen. It would've killed Mother. That's what Father said. We had to keep it from her."

"So you buried her in the basement?"

Max hung his head. "Yes."

"What about Felix?"

His face darkened. "Felix was fine and dandy. He'd run off days before."

"But...why haven't you told anyone since?" Andy asked.

"I couldn't. The longer I waited, the more impossible it became. I nearly managed to make myself believe it didn't happen. Maybe it was something I saw in a movie. Then you showed up, digging up the past."

"I've never thought you killed anyone. I still don't."

I had never seen eyes as haunted as Max's at that moment. "I'm not sure she was dead when we put her in the ground." He buried his face into his hands again.

Andy and I stared at him, unable to utter a word.

"That's quite the story," Lipkin's voice broke the silence. He stood at the top of the stairs, looking down at us.

***

Lipkin's arrival set the wheels of law and order in motion. There were statements to take, the basement to be dug up, lawyers to haggle with each other. Aside from our own account of the events, Andy I were not privy to any of it. We caught bits and pieces from the news. Meanwhile, our lives hopped back on their tracks with shocking ease.

I met Kevin in the same Starbucks on the morning of the twenty-fourth. The scent of cinnamon hung heavily in the air.

"How are you holding up?" I asked.

"I'm fine," he replied in a tone that made it obvious he wasn't fine.

"Leander and I are making a little dinner. Why don't you—"

"No offense, but the last thing I want is to spend Christmas Eve with you and your spooky boyfriend. I'll be with my sister. Family to the rescue." He snorted. "Max has his brother now."

"Felix?"

"Yes, apparently the world-traveling Felix has been back in California for years, living in Ojai. They weren't on speaking terms because Max didn't forgive him for running away, but now...blood thicker than water, and all that crap."

"So you talked to Max?"

Kevin nodded. "Briefly. They let him out on bail on the kidnapping charges, and the other stuff might not even go to court, seeing how he was a minor at the time. He'll be seeing a shrink though. Oh yeah, and he broke up with me."

"Oh. That's...unexpected."

He rubbed his face, and I got a glanced of the exhaustion, frustration and jumble of other emotions, before he pulled himself together.

"Hm. I don't know if I should be furious or relieved. Or who I should be pissed at. Right now you two are not not my favorite people." He glanced at his watch. "Look, I promised my sis to get there early and help."

"Okay. Call me if you need anything." I would've liked to help him sort out his troubles, but clearly I wasn't the right person.

He gave me a doubtful look and left.

***

I filled Andy in about Max and Felix later that day.

"This has been by far the strangest Christmas of my life," Andy said, while grating the zest off an orange.

"Which part, almost getting killed, or actually participating in the cooking process?"

"Both, I guess. And Max didn't really want to kill me. He panicked. He would've let me go. I know it."

I didn't want to argue with him about the subject again, so kept my mouth shut.

Andy put the orange down. "I'm done. Now what?"

"Mix it into the flour. Make sure it's not clumpy. Use your hands if you have to. They're clean, right?"

"Of course they are. Damn, you're like General Patton in the kitchen."

We worked side-by-side, saying few words till we transformed eggs, chocolate, flour, and butter into a dark gooey mass and poured it into the baking form.

"Yum." Andy licked the spatula with a satisfied expression.

Cake safely in the oven, I set the timer and pulled Andy to me. As we stood arms around each other, I felt more at peace than I had in a long time. "When I was a kid, we had a tradition that you could open one present early. What do you say? Would you like an early present?"

His face lit up. "That's an excellent tradition!"

"It's in my bedroom."

His hands slipped lower on my hips. "Is it something kinky?"

"Depends on your definition of kink," I replied, breaking our embrace. "Come on, decide for yourself."

Once in my room, I lifted the blanket hiding the surprise. "Here it is. Merry Christmas."

Andy clapped his hands together. "Lumber! Just what I've always wanted. How did you know?" He gave me one of those smiles that said I was a lovable lummox.

"It's a bookcase for your room, smart-ass. We'll build it together."

The smile fell off his face. "Right now?"

"Sure. Why not?"

"Don't you need tools for that?"

"I have everything. Don't worry, I've done this before. We have nothing better to do while the cake bakes."

"I could think of something better," he replied looking pointedly at the bed.

"Bookcase now, sex later."

"You're hot when you're bossy."

At the sight of the sparkles of mischief in his eyes a funny kind of warmth unfurled in my chest. That day, driving to Max's house, I thought what I'd find there would kill me, but instead it jump-started my heart. The poor old thing now beat in fear I could lose him, but also with joy for having him in my life.

I must have looked at him funny, because he tilted his head just so. "What?"

"Nothing," I said and stole a bittersweet kiss.

About the Author

Under a prickly, cynical surface Lou Harper is an incorrigible romantic. Her love affair with the written word started at a tender age. There was never a time when stories weren't romping around in her head. She is currently embroiled in a ruinous romance with adjectives. In her free time Lou stalks deviant words and feral narratives.

Lou's favorite animal is the hedgehog. She likes nature, books, movies, photography, and good food. She has a temper and mood swings.

Lou has misspent most of her life in parts of Europe and the US, but is now firmly settled in Los Angeles and worships the sun. However, she thinks the ocean smells funny. Lou is a loner, a misfit, and a happy drunk.

Web site: http://louharper.com
Blog: http://louharper.blogspot.com

Printed in Poland
by Amazon Fulfillment
Poland Sp. z o.o., Wrocław